I0601206

Josh Martin

Space Commander

M. L. Hollinger

Mouse Gate Series

Mouse Gate.
1103 Middlecreek
Friendswood, Texas 77546
281-992-3131   281-482-5390 Fax
www.mousegate.com

ISBN: 978-1-59095-282-5
UPC: 6-43977-62820-6

Library of Congress Control Number: 2015944693

Printed in the United States of America with simultaneous printings in Australia, Canada, and United Kingdom.

FIRST EDITION
1   2   3   4   5   6   7   8   9   10

To all teen-aged boys with little brothers
and to the memory of my own
little brother

Author M. L. Hollinger

 received an Aeronautical Engineering degree from Purdue University in 1957 and went into the Air Force right after college. He worked on several space program projects including; Titan III Space Booster, Space Shuttle, Star Wars and several other special studies for the Air Force. He attended the Air Command and Staff College and the Air War College. He served in Viet Nam from 1971-1972. His decorations include The Bronze Star Medal, Meritorious Service Medal, Air Force Commendation Medal, The Vietnamese Honor Medal First Class, The Vietnamese Gallantry Cross and five unit excellence awards. He retired from the Air Force in 1980 with the rank of Lieutenant Colonel and came back to Indiana where he joined the Indiana Corporation for Science and Technology. He is now fully retired.

Introduction

Josh Martin is forced to take care of his little brother on a family trip to Walt Disney World while his parents attend a sales convention there. The trip interrupts Josh's plans to date a girl he's been drooling over the whole school year. He also feels he's outgrown the theme park's attractions. While waiting in line at Space Mountain, Buzz Lightyear gives Josh a pin and promises he'll enjoy the ride much more this time. Josh experiences a strange adventure while on the ride. It seems to take days, but when the ride ends he awakens to find he's slept through the ride. It had to be a dream, but it seemed so real.

CHAPTER 1

Friday night was the only night Josh Martin dreaded. It was family dinner night, and he was forced to sit at the table enduring inane small talk for nearly an hour before he was released to the sanctuary of his room and the bliss of online gaming. Tonight was different, however, since it would be the beginning of his campaign of good behavior aimed at prying the keys to one of the family's cars out of his father's hands.

He needed a car for his date with Carolyn Forrest. He'd been asking her out for the last month, but she always had some excuse for turning him down. She finally said 'yes' after algebra class on Thursday, and in a little over a week all of his dreams would come true. He sat down next to his little brother, George and greeted his parents.

"Hi Mom, Dad. What's for dinner?"

His mother returned from the kitchen range with a platter of barbequed ribs. "Your Father's favorite tonight. He's got an important announcement to make," she said. She smiled that special conspiratorial smile only lovers know, and her husband returned the unspoken communication.

Josh knew such behavior always preceded something he didn't want to hear. What adults considered good news was often disastrous for teens. *Oh God, what now? This stuff always means something nerdy's going to happen,* Josh thought.

"After we say Grace, darling," his father replied.

The mandatory rote prayer finished, and the family turned its attention to the head of the table.

Warren Martin leaned back in his chair smiling broadly. "Well, you're looking at Universal Life's top salesman in the southeast district for the last quarter."

Good for you, Dad, but so what?

This news producing no spontaneous joyful response, Warren continued, "First of all, that means a nice bonus in the next paycheck, but best of all, the quarterly awards conference will be at Walt Disney World in Florida."

George squealed with glee, but Josh was not impressed. The family visited the theme park three years ago. It was fun then, but he'd outgrown it.

"When are we going?   When are we going?" George pleaded.

"That's the best part," Warren said.   "A week from tomorrow."

"That's great!" George said.

"Jeez Dad, I can't go **then**," Josh said.

"Why not?" his mother asked.

"I've got a date next Saturday night. I've been asking this girl out for weeks, and she finally said yes. I can't go."

"If she said yes now, she'll say yes again, son.   This opportunity is here and now," his father said.

"I'm sure she'll understand once you explain it to her," his mother added.

"I've outgrown Disney World, Dad. Can't I stay here while you guys go?"

Warren looked at his wife who shook her head emphatically

to reinforce his own opinion of the request. "I'm sorry, but that's not an option. Besides, you need to be there to take care of your little brother while your mother and I are busy at company functions. We're all going, and that's final. Now eat your dinner."

CHAPTER 2

The drive from Savannah to Orlando took over six hours due to George's required stops for restrooms and snacks. The hotel at least had a big swimming pool, and Josh took advantage of the afternoon sun and warm water while his parents unpacked. He needed something to soften the blow of shepherding his little brother through the Magic Kingdom while they attended the first banquet on their schedule.

As he sunned himself on a chaise lounge, he studied the clientele. It was mostly sub-teen kids and their parents. *Not one hot babe in sight. What a waste of time. When I think of what I could be doing tonight if I was back home. Oh Carolyn, I sure hope you don't give up on me because of this. She seemed to be okay with it, but you never know about girls. Instead of hanging out with her I'll be standing in line with my little brother waiting for a dumb ride.*

His mother's voice interrupted his thoughts. "Come in now, Josh. It's time for you to get ready to take your brother to the Magic Kingdom."

"Okay, I'm coming." He followed his mother back to the hotel rooms and dressed for the afternoon. George was already anxious to get to the rides.

"Hey Bro, make it quick. The lines are a mile long this time of day."

"Take it easy. We've got all weekend." Josh didn't feel like he really needed a shower, but he took one just to torment his brother.

* * * * * *

The bus dropped Josh and George off at the entrance to the Magic Kingdom, and George immediately made his preferences known.

"Let's get over to Space Mountain first. I don't care much about the other stuff, but I don't want to miss that, and the lines are always long."

"Whatever you want." Josh escorted his brother through the shops and stores of Main Street USA to Tomorrowland where the line for Space Mountain was every bit as long as they'd expected.

"Look at that! We'll be here for hours," Josh said.

"It goes fast. Come on, get in line."

As they stood there Buzz Lightyear came up to entertain the waiting crowd.

"Over here, Buzz!" George shouted, and the character responded immediately. He shook George's hand and posed with him while Josh snapped a picture with his cell phone. Josh was surprised when the character spoke to him.

"You look very bored. Here, take this and pin it on your shirt. It'll make the ride much more enjoyable." He handed him a simple pin much like a political campaign button. Instead of some politician's picture it bore a black circle with mouse ears on a white background. He stared at it while Buzz moved on to other patrons.

"What'd he give you?" George grabbed for the button, but Josh pulled it away.

"Just a dumb button."

"Give it to me!"

"No, he gave it to me, and I'm keeping it." Josh didn't really want the button, but he enjoyed teasing his brother about it too much to let him have it.

"Why didn't he give me one?"

"I don't know. Maybe you're too young?"

George turned away to sulk. "That's okay, I'll buy one in the gift shop."

Josh pinned the button on his shirt and shuffled forward in the line until it was their turn to board the ride.

"Oh, I see Buzz gave you one of our special buttons," the cast member seating them pointed to Josh's button.

"Yeah, do I get a special discount, or something?"

The cast member laughed. "No, but I think you'll enjoy the ride much more."

Josh didn't notice him pressing a button on the side of the sled as it moved away from the boarding area.

The sled seemed to accelerate to a phenomenal speed. Streaks of red and blue light flashed past as they sped toward a white glare. Josh looked where his brother should have been, but he was alone. *What's going on here? This can't be part of the ride. Something's wrong.*

Suddenly, the kaleidoscope of color vanished, and he found himself in a scene out of a science fiction movie. Men and women in futuristic uniforms worked consoles and moved about the room in a businesslike manner. A large screen in front of him showed a pattern of stars on a black background. *Am I dreaming? Did I fall asleep? How could I? This ride really shakes you up. There's no way I could be asleep, but what's this if it isn't a dream?*

He looked at his hands and saw his father's hands. He was also in the same type uniform as the others, yet he was doing nothing while they were busy performing whatever tasks they were responsible for. One of the men approached him and spoke. "Commander, the ship is on course for Gabba Three as you ordered. Is there anything else?"

How is it I know this guy's name? He's my Executive Officer, Bob Blake. What do I tell him? Oh well, do what they do on the TV shows. "That's all for now. Carry on."

"Yes, sir." He turned and took his seat at one of the consoles.

I'm the commander of a space ship. I wonder what kind it is? He studied the buttons on his chair's armrests and found he knew what each one was for. *This is really weird! I think this one'll tell me what I'm the commander of.* He touched the button pad, and the screen changed to show the profile of a large spaceship. The caption read, "Royal Truvian Space Force Battle Cruiser Ares."

Oh my God! This is some kind of warship. He touched the button pad again, and the screen changed to a display of the ship's weaponry. The list included: four 100 gigawatt laser cannon, sixteen 250 megawatt photon guns, 100 half-megaton multi-guidance missiles, 300 space mines, six FA-493 fighter craft and three shuttle craft. *Wow! What power!*

He touched the button pad again, and this time it showed the ship's crew roster. Each group's listing showed the total number of personnel authorized, the number aboard and a summary of their status. The flying group was fully manned, but 20% of them were on sick call. The missile group was only 90% staffed, but only one man was ill. A company of Royal Marines was aboard totaling six officers and 108 enlisted men.

Another touch produced a listing of the ship's systems. He selected propulsion, and a diagram of the engines appeared showing all sub-systems running normally. He continued through several other screens he didn't understand until the star pattern returned.

Awesome! This is better than any computer game. Maybe I should try some stuff? He was about to experiment when the Executive Officer approached again.

"Sir, we just received a message from Royal Space Force Headquarters. It's on channel five."

Josh looked at his controls again and found the button for the communications screen. In short order a stern face appeared.

"This is Admiral Goodwin. The Princess Ariadne has been kidnapped by the Dilurian pirates. They are holding her for ransom on their home planet of Dilura. Your assignment is to rescue the Princess and destroy the pirates. I regret we are unable to release any other warships to assist you in this mission. Time is of the essence. The pirates have threatened to kill her unless the ransom is paid within seven Dilurian days. Good luck."

The screen went blank. Josh sat for a moment staring at the dead display. *What am I supposed to do about that? I'm not a spaceship commander. I don't even know how I got here in the first place.* Executive Officer Blake broke in.

"Shall I set course for Dilura, sir?"

I gotta stop this now. "Hey, you guys, I'm not your commander. I'm Josh Martin. I'm just a kid. I don't know anything about this stuff." He swept his hands across the consoles and displays on what he now knew was the bridge.

Blake looked at him calmly. "It's all right, Commander. We understand, but this is no time for one of your tantrums. We've been assigned a very important mission, and we need to get going. Might I suggest a staff meeting?"

"No, you don't understand. I'm just on a silly ride at Disney World. I'm only sixteen years old. I can't do this."

The click of keyboards grew silent as all the crew on the bridge turned to stare at him. Blake continued. "You wear the badge of the royal space force and the insignia of a Commander in that force. You've commanded this ship for the last four years. Snap out of it, sir!" He pointed to Josh's chest, and Josh followed his finger to the badge. It was a silver circle with mouse ears. He leaned close to Josh and whispered in his ear. "You have a great crew. Call a staff meeting to develop a plan of action. Meanwhile, we can start for Dilura. Just tell the helmsman to set the course."

Oh my God! This is wild. I guess I'd better play along with this for a while. What would Captain Kirk say? I got it. "Okay, helmsman, set a course for Dilura."

"Yes, sir," a man at a nearby console responded.

That was pretty easy, now for the other part. "I call a staff meeting now in..." He turned to Blake and whispered, "Where?"

Blake responded in a whisper, "The briefing room, sir."

"In the briefing room." Once more he consulted Blake, "Where's that?"

"Follow me, sir."

Blake led him to a conference room and indicated his chair. Josh sat, and Blake sat next to him. The other officers filed in and took their seats. All eyes turned toward Josh. *What am I supposed to say? What would I do if this were a computer game? I know.* "What do we know about these Dilurian pirates?"

A female officer at the other end of the table rose. She pointed a device at a screen, and a map appeared. "Sir, this is a map of the area around the pirate's stronghold. As you can see, it's situated on a large island in the middle of one of the planet's oceans. Dilura is a very primitive planet. The people have not progressed much beyond their bronze age. The pirates are originally from Festa, but they were forced to leave when the government there outlawed piracy. They came here and enslaved the native people of this island. The slaves work the farms which supply the pirates with most of their food. They import the things they can't grow. I should say they steal them. They prey on merchant shipping for most of their needs and for money to buy what they can't capture. They're a treacherous, evil lot with no morals at all." She sat down.

Blake spoke up. "What is their military capability?"

A young officer seated on Josh's right rose and changed the display. "Sir, they have ten converted merchant ships armed with mid-power laser cannon and short range missiles. They attack merchants with three or more ships causing them to surrender their cargo rather than risk a fight. They are no match for any warship larger than a destroyer."

"Could they do us any damage?" Josh asked.

"If they attacked with their full force, they could overwhelm our defensive systems until we destroyed at least four of them. In that time they could cause some minor damage. It's very doubtful they would have their entire fleet available at any one time. Maintenance problems and ships deployed to intercept freighters probably cut the home fleet down considerably."

"Where would they be holding the princess?" Josh asked.

A more senior officer rose to answer that question. "In my

opinion they wouldn't be holding her on their orbital docking station. It's pretty primitive, being a captured freighter converted into a dock. I'd say they'd have her at their fortress on the island. They keep a contingent of pirates there at all times in case of attack from the sea. It's a pretty formidable installation. They have some heavy laser cannon and numerous short range missiles in their arsenal."

Josh found himself feeling more and more comfortable in the situation. He didn't have to know anything. All he had to do was ask the other officers for inputs. *Hey, why don't they just pay off the pirates?* "How much ransom are these pirates asking for?" he said.

A junior officer answered. "One billion credits, sir."

"Jeez, that's peanuts for any big government. What's the big deal?"

Blake leaned close to him. "Sir, if the King's Council wanted to pay it, they would have done that by now. We have to find some other approach."

Okay, so they won't pay up. We'll just go in there and blast 'em. "I guess we'll just have to attack as soon as we get there," Josh said.

"It's not that easy," Blake said.

"Why's that? We've got 'em outgunned from what you guys tell me," Josh said.

"The pirates have threatened to execute the princess if we attack," Blake said. "We can't risk it."

There must be some way to get to those bozos. "What do they want the money for?"

The room fell silent as everyone turned to stare at Josh. The older officer was the first to comment. "That's a good question."

"I never thought of that," another said.

"I don't suppose they have any kind of retirement plan they're saving for," the female said, drawing a ripple of laughter from the staff.

"They definitely need to buy fuel for their ships plus missiles and gases for their cannons," a balding officer commented.

"I also understand the pirates are very fond of pork, and there are no pigs on Dilura. It has to be imported," another officer added.

"Why couldn't they import some pigs and raise their own meat?" Josh asked.

This caused a sidebar conference between the female officer and another young officer. The rest of the staff watched and waited for the result. The female officer finally spoke.

"Sir, they tried that once and the native slaves wouldn't care for the pigs. They were deathly afraid of the animals for some reason."

Hey, I've seen this plot before in movies. We sneak in disguised as something else and free the princess while our ship destroys the pirates. Maybe pork's the key. Wait a minute, we can't go in as canned hams. What could we do? Maybe if I suggest something, the staff'll figure out the details for me.

"We can use the pork thing to get the job done." Josh said. "We send in a small group posing as pork traders and arrange for the sale of a shipload of pork. The agents could find out where the princess is and come up with a way to rescue her."

"Good idea," the older officer said. "The pork would have to go to the island. They wouldn't leave it on the orbital dock. We could hide our marines in the shipping containers, and they could attack after they reach the island."

"Won't it be cold inside those containers?" Josh asked.

"That's no problem. They could wear cold weather gear, and they'd only have to be in the containers for a short while," another officer said.

"I think you've got something there, Commander," the older officer said. "We send a delegation to the pirates aboard a civilian ship to negotiate the pork deal. They find the princess and work out a plan to keep her safe. We load the marines aboard the freighter. When our agents on the island tell us they're ready, we send in the pork ship with the marines aboard. The marines land and start blasting the pirates while this ship takes care of the home fleet. We destroy their ships and turn our weapons on the island, if needed."

"It could work," Blake said. "But, we have to find a freighter full of pork."

Hey, looks like we've got a plan. Maybe this is all I need to get me out of this mess. "Okay, let's get with it," Josh said.

The meeting broke up into smaller groups, and Blake leaned closer to Josh. "Good job, Commander.

CHAPTER 3

As the staff consulted their computers and conferenced in small groups, Blake turned to Josh. "It shouldn't take long for the staff to figure it all out. We'll just wait here while they work. Are you over your little tantrum now, sir?"

"It wasn't a tantrum. I'm only a kid, not a spaceship commander. I was on the Space Mountain ride with my little brother when I suddenly found myself here."

"Well, whatever. You're doing a good job so far. Keep it up."

In a few moments an officer entered and spoke to Josh, "Sir, the Bremen freighter Belarius is nearby and has offered to help. She's carrying supplies for a mining operation on Rigna II including five metric tons of pork products. She has two shuttle craft capable of reaching Dilura from here and will loan one to us. The Captain says he has several empty containers aboard, and we could load the marines in those. The problem is each one of the shuttles can only carry four containers."

The Marine commander spoke. "We could only get about six men in full combat gear in each container, sir."

"Well, that means a change of plans," Blake said. He called the room to attention. "Listen up everyone. We have a freighter, but it can only land 24 marines. We need to get the whole company down quickly to maintain surprise. If the orbital port gets off a warning, their fortress missiles will blast the shuttle craft before we can land enough people to do the job. Any ideas?"

The female officer spoke up. "Sir, their only anti-space missiles are in the fortress. If we have control of it, we could commandeer whatever shuttle craft are available at the docking station."

"Thank you, Lieutenant. We can't go into full attack mode until we know the Princess is safe, and the fortress's missiles are secure," Blake said. "Do you have any suggestions, Captain?"

"Me?" Josh looked around the room. *Why is everyone looking at me? I don't know anything about this stuff. Looks like I'm going to have to come up with something, though. Let's see, what would Captain Kirk do? I know.* "I leave the details to you staff people. Let's get going."

The staff began to confer with each other. They studied computer screens and the female officer finally spoke. "Sir, won't the pirates insist the initial party be unarmed?"

"The Belarius is a Bremen ship, and Bremens insist on carrying their pistols at all times. Asking them to leave their side arms behind would be a deal breaker," Blake said.

"I don't think the pirates would worry about a few men with laser pistols taking over their fortress," Major Burns said.

"Where do I fit into all this?" Josh asked.

"You'll go in with the initial party and find the Princess. It'll be up to you to figure out a way to keep her safe while we attack," Blake said. "You're the one who'll have to make the final decision, and you can do it much better if you're on the scene."

"Whoa, wait a minute. How many pirates are we talking about?" Josh asked.

The more senior officer spoke, "That depends on how many of their ships are out on the hunt when we get there. If most of them are on patrol, there should only be two or three hundred on the island."

"And, how many marines can we get on the shuttle craft?" Josh asked.

The female officer spoke, "If the Belarius' shuttles are the usual model, maybe six, including the pilot."

"What can six of us do to keep the Princess safe against two or three hundred pirates?" Josh asked.

"Five marines can go in with you to help, and one of them will pose as the Captain of the Belarius. We'll keep the freighter away until you signal us the Princess is safe, then we'll go in," Blake said.

At that point the intercom broke in. "Freighter Belarius is now on station with us and requesting permission to dock."

Blake punched a communicator button. "Go ahead with docking." He turned to Josh. "You need to have Major Burns pick the Marines to accompany you, sir."

"Okay. Major Burns."

"Yes, sir."

"Please pick five of your men to accompany me to the pirate stronghold on Dilura."

Blake leaned closer and whispered, "Don't forget one has to pose as the Captain of the Belarius."

"Oh, I almost forgot. One of them has to pretend he's the Captain of the Belarius."

"That's easy, sir. Lieutenant Rodgers is very familiar with that class of ship. He could do it easily," Burns said.

The Major left the room just as the intercom spoke again. "The Belarius is docked, and Captain Rollus requests permission to come aboard."

Blake fixes Josh in a questioning look, and Josh gets the message. "Oh yeah, tell him it's okay." Blake points to the conference table, and again, Josh gets it. "Send him to the briefing room."

A few moments later the biggest man Josh had ever seen walks into the briefing room. He is well over two meters tall and very heavily built. He wears a black tunic over skin-tight dark gray pants ending in polished black boots. A wide leather belt around his waist holds a formidable-looking knife and a laser pistol holster. A silver badge over his left breast pocket catches Josh's eye. It's an intricate pattern of star shapes, and he guesses it identifies him as the freighter's Captain. Blake rises as he enters, and Josh follows suit.

"I am Rollus, Captain of the Belarius," the visitor announces.

"Welcome Captain Rollus," Blake said as he nudged Josh with his elbow.

"Oh yeah, welcome Captain Rollus. Please have a seat." He noticed Blake nodding approval.

They sat, and Blake explained the mission to Rollus.

"I see, I'm proud to help free the Princess. We Bremens love her as much as you do, and we'd hate to see any harm come to her. I only see a few problems with your plan."

"What's that?" Josh said.

"First, since you will be placing one of my shuttle craft in jeopardy, I assume the Crown will reimburse me for its loss or any repairs it may require."

"You can be sure of that," Blake answered.

"Second, I don't see how you can pass off any of your men as Bremens. I haven't seen anyone on your ship the pirates would believe."

Blake buzzed the intercom for Major Burns.

"Yes, sir," he answered.

"Burns, have you selected the Marines for the mission?"

"Yes, sir. We're ready to go."

"Bring them into the briefing room, please."

"Be right there, sir."

"I think you'll be pleasantly surprised by these men, Captain," Blake said.

Burns returned leading a group of men every bit as large as Captain Rollus.

"I see what you mean. Yes, these men could be mistaken for Bremens. We can easily find clothes for them among my crew," Rollus said.

"I selected them for their size as well as their skill with weapons," Burns said.

"But there are only five of them. Who is the sixth man?" Rollus asked.

"The Commander will be going with them also," Blake said.

Rollus looked at Josh and a smile spread across his face. "I think our cabin boy's uniform will fit the Commander."

"Hey, I may be a kid inside, but this is a man's body," Josh said.

"I beg your pardon, Commander. I meant no disrespect. It's only that Bremens are a large race, and even a man of your obvious strength and size is small in comparison."

"I guess it's okay," Josh said.

"The last problem I have is with one of your men impersonating me. I've done business with Sorbius, the pirate King, before. He knows me. I'm afraid I'll have to go with you and do the negotiating with him while your men find where he's holding the Princess."

"I hate to put you in jeopardy too," Blake said.

"I will have no trouble with the pirates. In fact, my presence will make your job much easier. You may release one of your men, Major."

Burns turned to the smallest of his Marines, "You can stay here, Carlson."

Carlson's face turned into a sour expression, but he saluted and left the room.

Blake spoke, "Have you filled the men in on the mission, Major Burns?"

"Yes, sir, we're set to go."

"Whenever you're ready Commander," Blake said to Josh.

"Yeah, let's get with it. Lead the way Captain Rollus," Josh said.

They left the Ares and boarded the Belarius. Josh observed that everything on the freighter seemed to be sized for Bremens. The companionways were a good 20 centimeters higher than the Ares, and all the controls were at his shoulder level. Rollus led them to a wardroom where other men waited with clothing and weapons.

"These men will help outfit your people, Commander. Who will be piloting the shuttle craft?"

A red-headed Sargent raised his hand. "I will, Captain."

"Good. I'll check you out on the controls once you've changed clothes."

One of the Bremens approached Josh. "Well, Commander, I see we'll have to find some smaller items for you."

"The boss said you'd get me the cabin boy's outfit," Josh replied.

The Bremen laughed. "I'm afraid even he may be too big for you, but I'll find something. Be right back." He left Josh alone with his thoughts. *How am I going to find the Princess? If I find her, how do we keep the pirates from killing her? This is all way over my head. These guys know what they're doing, but I haven't got a clue. Why don't I just wake up? The ride must have been over a long time ago, but I'm still here. What do I have to do to get back? I could be killed doing this. What'll happen to me then? I'm inside this guy's body, but if he's killed will I still be around back home, or do I die too?* He picked up a laser pistol and studied it. *I wonder how this thing works. It looks like a regular gun. Let's see, I've seen guys work this kind of thing on television. They pull back on this thing here to start it.* He worked the slide, and the click brought every eye in the room in his direction. The Marine closest to him reacted first.

"Easy, Commander. That thing's loaded." He carefully lifted Josh's arm to point the pistol at the ceiling eliciting several sighs of relief. "I'm sure you're not familiar with these Breman weapons. Let me show you how to use it. Now that you've armed it, sir, you have to either fire it or disarm it. You disarm it by holding this button down and working the slide again." He disarmed the pistol and pointed Josh toward a bare wall. "Try it for yourself, sir."

Josh pulled back the slide, and the room grew silent again. He pushed down on the button and worked the slide. "I see how it goes now. I suppose once you've pulled back on that thingy all you have to do is pull the trigger to fire it." Several stifled snickers told Josh he'd used the wrong term for the slide.

"Yes, sir. The energy pack should be enough for this mission, but if you have to change it, you simple push that button and the old pack will be ejected. Just shove a new one into the grip to fire again. This lever is the safety." He pointed to a small lever near the trigger.

Josh experimented with the pistol until the Bremen came back with some clothes for him. "Try these on, sir."

Josh took the clothes and noticed they were brand new. "These are new. Do you have a store aboard?"

"No, sir. These belong to Samson. He bought them for his son before we left our last port."

Josh put on the clothes after removing the price tags. They fit him perfectly. "How old is Samson's son?" he asked.

"He's 13 in Earth years, sir." Once more a ripple of muffled laughter spread through the room.

"Big for his age, I guess," Josh said.

"Yes, sir," the Bremen answered, not wanting to pursue the conversation further.

Lieutenant Rodgers spoke, "We're ready to go as soon as Sargent Bowers is checked out on the shuttlecraft."

"Okay, relax until he gets back, guys." The men reacted to Josh's casual tone, but followed the order willingly. It wasn't long until Rollus and Bowers returned.

"I'm all checked out, Lieutenant. I guess we're ready now," Bowers said.

"With your permission, sir," Rodgers addressed Josh.

"Yeah, let's go," Josh said.

Rollus led the group to the shuttlecraft, and the party went aboard. It was loaded with spare energy packs for the laser pistols and a few rations. Josh took a seat and buckled in while the pilot started the engines. The hatch of the freighter opened, and the craft rose into dark space.

"One hour to Dilura, sir," Rodgers said over the whine of the engines.

CHAPTER 4

Lieutenant Rodgers handed Josh a tiny earpiece and microphone all in one unit. "Put on this headset, sir, so you can hear what's going on up front." He plugged the cord into Josh's left armrest. "Just press this button to talk." He pointed to a red button on the same armrest.

There was no radio traffic to listen to, and Josh pondered his situation for the hundredth time. *I don't know what's going on, but it looks like I'll have to play along with it until something happens that'll send me back home. The only way I can think to play this is like it's a computer game. There aren't any icons I can click on, and there's no way to do anything but through this body I'm in. Hey, I know, the body's just like an input thing. I don't need a mouse, this guy can do what I tell him to. I don't need to scroll the screen, I just have to look around. Hey, this is really awesome, come to think of it.*

"Shuttlecraft approaching Dilura, identify yourself."

The rough, threatening voice shocked Josh into the present. Rollus' voice answered. "Tell Sorbius that Rollus has a deal for him on some pork. We'll be at your docking port in 45 minutes. I also have some prospective recruits for him from Brem. I know he likes to get all the Bremens he can. Do you want us to stop at the docking port, or can we go straight to the island?"

A short silence followed, and Josh guessed the operator at the docking port was checking with the pirate King.

"We're being painted with missile radar signals from some ships in orbit around Dilura," Sargent Bowers said.

"Just routine, Sergeantt," Rollus assured him.

"It's okay, Captain Rollus, the boss says you can go to the island," the docking port replied.

"Thanks. You hungry for some bacon?" Rollus said.

"You're just in time, we're almost out, and none of the ships we've taken lately have any in their stores. Your stuff will be a welcome sight, whatever the price."

Rollus turned and gave Josh a "thumbs up" sign. He smiled broadly as he removed his headset and turned to Lieutenant Rodgers. "I hope you didn't mind me telling them your men were prospective recruits? It's the only way you'll get to see all of the stronghold. Sorbius may send a man with you as a guide, but once you find the Princess you can overpower him and do whatever it takes to keep her safe while your ship launches the attack."

"What about you, Captain?" Josh asked. "Won't Sorbius know you've tricked him as soon as the action starts?"

"Hopefully, I'll be out of his reach when the fighting begins."

"I hope you know what you're doing," Josh said.

The shuttlecraft landed at the island spaceport, and a delegation waited for them. Rollus stepped out first to the music of the Brem planetary anthem played by a rag-tag band of pirates using instruments depicting the variety of ships they'd plundered. A group of women clad in very skimpy outfits danced provocatively on one side while a dubious-looking honor guard arrayed in a hodge-podge of uniforms stood at a lazy version of attention. There was, however, nothing shoddy about the man who moved to embrace the Captain.

He wore a white silk shirt tucked into a red sash around his waist. Tight black pants ended in highly polished black boots. His long black hair ended just above his shoulders, and the one exposed ear sported a large gold loop earring. He carried no weapons except for a very ornate dagger hanging from a belt hidden by his sash. The clean-shaven face was handsome by any standard. Josh thought all he needed to fulfill the stereotype of the pirate was a patch over one eye. Two burly bodyguards stood two paces behind him, and a smaller man in business clothes hovered on his left side.

"Welcome to my island, Rollus. I hope you're bringing us some good food as well as these wonderful recruits," he said.

Rollus kissed the pirate King on both cheeks before dropping his embrace. "I have all you could want, friend, but we need to go someplace where we can discuss the matter with less background noise." He waved a hand at the band and the ladies dancing and slapping their tambourines. "Do you mind if these men take a look around your stronghold?" He indicated the marines posing as Bremens.

"Not at all. If they have any questions, they can ask any pirate they see. They'll contact me if they can't answer." Sorbius spoke to the marines. "We'll meet in my suite for lunch in two hours. You can tell me if you're interested in life as a pirate then. Any questions for me now?"

Hey, this is my chance, Josh thought before he spoke. "Mr. Pirate King, I have a question."

Sorbius looked at Josh for the first time and noticed he was smaller than the rest. "Are you a Bremen?" he asked.

"Yeah, but I'm a dwarf Bremen." He felt that might be an acceptable explanation, but it only drew derisive laughter from everyone around him.

"What is your question, small Bremen?"

"I heard you've captured a royal princess. I'd like to see her. I've never seen a princess before." More laughter met this statement.

Sorbius recovered enough to speak. "A strange request, but if that's what it will take to convince you to join us, you're welcome to visit her." He turned to one of his bodyguards. "Magran, show this man the Princess."

The bodyguard stepped forward, and Josh immediately saw the man wasn't happy with the assignment. "This way," was his only conversation.

Josh followed him into a street lined with stalls selling anything a pirate could want. A tobacco display complete with pipes and cigars filled the air with aromatic smoke, but it competed with the food stall across from it. A jewelry vendor hawked his wares extolling the quality of his gems. Further down a coffee shop spiced the atmosphere. His guide moved on in silence to a cross street where they left the bazaar and entered a nearly deserted area.

Josh thought this a good time to try engaging Magran in conversation. "Hey, Magran, what do you like about being a pirate?"

Magran didn't turn to face Josh or alter his stride. "The money's good."

"No, I mean what is it about this life that brought you into it in the first place?"

"It was a way to escape the hot breath of the law on the back of my neck."

"Oh? Why were they after you?"

"I murdered three men in a bar brawl, and they didn't buy my version of the story."

"Why not?"

"I told the law the three guys charged into my knife. They said they'd believe one time, but six times was stretching things too far for them. So, I took off and joined the pirates."

"Where do you go from here?"

"There ain't no 'from here'. This is the end of the line for a guy like me."

They walked on in silence toward a large stone wall with an iron door. The wall rose a good 15 meters, and there were no windows. Firing slots were the only openings in the black, rough surface. Josh guessed this might be the pirate's place for a last stand. "This is a pretty awesome fortress. Is it a jail?"

"Nope, it's our fort of last resort. If we're attacked, and our ships can't fend off the bad guys, we all come here and hold out to the last man. The Princess is inside."

Magran knocked on the iron door, and a small window opened revealing a camera.

"Oh, it's you, Magran. Who's that with you?"

"He's okay. He's a prospective recruit. Just open up."

A mechanical noise and a loud click preceded the door opening a small crack. Magran pushed it open and led Josh inside.

The interior was as foreboding as the exterior. They stood in a small foyer facing another iron door. Josh noticed firing slots in each wall. Another click opened the next door where they were met by a heavily armed pirate with a red beard and shiny bald head.

"How is she today?" Magran asked.

"Same as last time, complaining constantly and yelling curses at anyone who passes her room."

"This guy's curious about what a princess looks like. Is she throwing things today?"

"I think she's thrown everything that's not nailed down by now, but Lyle just took a food tray to her and that hag of a maid we captured with her. She'll probably throw that stuff at you if you go up now."

"I'll show... What is your name, anyway?"

"Josh, my name's Josh." He didn't know what the Commander's name was, and he figured Magran might get suspicious if he used his rank.

"Okay, Josh, you need to see the rest of the place anyway. This way."

Magran led him down a hallway to some stairs and climbed to the roof of the fortress. The sun was almost overhead, and the heat was quite a contrast to the cool, damp interior. He hadn't noticed any ducts for air conditioning, and guessed the fortress was naturally that way—like a basement or a cave back home. Several pillboxes dotted the roof along with what he guessed were radomes of some kind. Margran explained, "This is our missile defense system. We got it from the Velusians in exchange for one of their ambassadors we captured. It'll handle almost anything built before last year. We feel pretty safe with it."

"I hear a Truvian battle cruiser has some pretty sophisticated missiles," Josh said.

"I don't think they'd be a problem. Come on downstairs, and I'll show you the arsenal."

He led Josh down to a room filled with weapons of all types, most of which Josh knew nothing about. He felt he should say something complimentary about the items, though.

"Pretty impressive. Looks like you've got one of about everything."

"One? We got over 100 of any kind of weapon you could ask for. We pull 'em off the ships we capture."

"By the way, what do you do with the ships you capture?"

"We usually just strip 'em bare of anything we can use and let 'em go on their way. We got no need for most of the ships themselves. If we get one we can convert to a warship pretty easy, we either send the crew off in one o' their shuttle craft or kill 'em off."

"Make 'em walk the plank, eh?"

Magran laughed heartily. "I guess you could say that. We use a more modern version, we just blow 'em out the airlock."

"If you have to spend some time here, where do you sleep, and what do you eat?"

"No worries there. This way to the barracks and mess hall." He led Josh through another corridor and down a flight of stairs to a large dormitory. Josh guessed they were now well under ground level. Inside he saw four men playing cards and three lying on bunks either reading or napping.

"How many men do you usually have here?" Josh asked.

"No more than twenty unless we're under high alert," Magran answered. "We'll move two hundred in if it looks like we're going to be attacked. The mess hall's this way." Josh followed him to a large room with long tables, a row of food synthesizers and a kitchen area.

"Pretty nice," Josh said. "How long can you hold out here?"

"As long as we like. Fresh water comes from a deep well

inside the fortress, and we can synthesize food, like on a spaceship, but we can bring in fresh food through the secret tunnel."

"Sounds interesting. Where's that?"

"Back this way."

They retraced their steps to a stairway leading down into darkness. Magran took an LED torch from a rack on the wall to light their way. At the bottom the stairs they faced a heavy wooden door. Thick wood slabs barred the top and bottom.

"How does anyone get in here from the other side?" Josh asked.

"There's an intercom in the tunnel. They just call up to the control center, and the guard on duty pulls back the bars. You can also do it from here." Magran opened a small cover to the right of the door and pushed a red button. The slabs retracted into the wall, and the door lifted up into the ceiling. A green button turned on the lights in the tunnel. "Have a look."

Josh peered into the door expecting to see stalactites, dripping water and a dirt floor, but found something more like the subway stations of New York City. The walls were tiled in white and ended at an arched ceiling of painted concrete. The concrete floor was freshly swept and showed no evidence of dampness. "Wow, really cool," Josh said.

"Yeah, it stays a steady 13ºC down here all the time."

"Sorry, I didn't mean the temperature. It's a Bremen expression meaning it's really awesome."

"Well, it's impressive, but awesome's a little over the top."

"Heh, heh, another Bremen expression. I meant it's very impressive. Say, what would you do if an enemy found the tunnel and tried to get in that way?"

"We'd see 'em on the cameras and blow the tunnel. You can do that from here, too. That red shield covers the destruct button. Break the wire holding it down, lift it up and push, and 'blam' the tunnel collapses on the bad guys."

"Looks like you guys've thought of everything."

"We've captured some good engineers and offered them their freedom for designing our stuff." Magran consulted his watch. "The Princess ought to be finished with her lunch by now. I'll take you back up to where you can have a look at her."

They climbed two flights of stairs to the fighting floor of the fortress. Laser cannon stood ready to be moved into position behind gun ports, and stocks of rifles and hand-held missiles lined the inner walls. Josh stopped. He suddenly realized everything he'd seen depended upon electricity.

"Say, what happens if the power goes out here?" Josh asked.

"Never happen. We got our own nuclear power plant three stories below the tunnel entrance. You'd have to have a very large fusion weapon to dig it out, and they're illegal."

"Don't you think the space force'd have no problem using nukes on pirates?"

"What? Those guys? We don't give a darn about the law, but they gotta follow it. Around this way."

To the left of the tunnel door a hallway led to two storage rooms. One was cellar temperature and contained casks of wine and boxes of items not requiring refrigeration. The other was cold storage with a freezer section in the rear. "We could hold out here forever if we wanted to," Magran said.

"Awesome," Josh said. "Has anyone ever tried to attack you?"

"Once or twice in the early days, but not lately. We keep

nearby governments happy by not attacking their ships. The ones farther out think it's too much trouble as long as we don't take too many of their ships."

"What about the Truvians?"

"You mean because we kidnapped one of their Princesses?"

"Yeah, won't they be mad about that?"

"Sorbius thinks they'll just pay up. We aren't asking that much ransom for her. Besides, they don't want to risk her life by attacking."

"Yeah, but if they attack, and you kill her, they'll have no reason to hold back, and you'll have no ransom money."

Magran smiled like one of Josh's teachers who just witnessed a student making his point for him. "That's why we didn't ask much ransom. Sure, they'd probably do a lot of damage, but they know they can't break into this fortress. They'd lose a lot of men and maybe a few warships in the process, and the cost of that's bigger than the ransom."

"Pretty slick." Josh checked his watch. "Say, we haven't got much time until lunch, and I'd still like to see a real princess."

"Okay, she's probably finished her late breakfast by now." Magran led Josh to an ornate door guarded by a pirate in servant's livery.

"Hey Magran, what's up?" the pirate asked.

"What's with the fancy outfit?" Magran asked.

"It's the Princess. She insists that anyone who comes into her digs is dressed in what she considers 'proper attire'. We dug this monkey suit out of some stuff we captured last week."

"On you it looks good," Magran said.

"Who's this?" the guard asked.

"This is Josh, a Bremen. He may be joining us, and he's

curious about what a real princess looks like."

"I'll say this one's worth taking a peek at, but she's a real hellion. You can try getting a look at her through the peephole, but she keeps that blocked most of the time, and if it isn't, she only throws something at it the minute she hears it opening."

"Let's try the peep hole first," Magran said.

The guard/servant stood to one side as he slid back the door covering the small window into the room. The only thing emerging from the space was a rather harsh voice. "Who's there?"

"The Princess has a visitor," Magran said.

A more seductive voice said, "Have him come to the window so I can see him."

Magran and the guard stood back and bowed toward the door while smiling at Josh like two pieces of bait in a hidden trap.

Josh moved to the door and ducked just as something sticky blasted through the opening. The softer voice said, "Now go away."

"They would give her crème brulèe this morning," the guard said.

Josh cautiously lifted his head to the window and saw a very lovely face looking back. She was about to throw another volley when her hand froze in mid-hurl. The other hand flew to her face, but failed to stifle a sharp gasp.

Magran said, "I guess she's never seen a Bremen close up."

The guard responded by holding back his laughter, and whispered to Magran, "This one's kind of a shrimp, for a Bremen, but I guess size don't matter for those guys."

"May I come in for a moment?" Josh said.

"Wh, wh, why certainly," she said.

The guard looked at Magran and back to Josh with an astonished expression. "She's never let anybody in that easy before," he said.

"I guess you gotta be a Bremen," Josh said. "You heard the lady, open up."

"I think I'd better keep this while you're in there." Magran removed Josh's laser pistol from its holster.

"Oh yeah, good idea," Josh said.

The guard opened the door, and Josh watched carefully as he entered four digits on the lock's keypad. *Four, six, one, eight—remember that, you'll need it later. Four, six, one, eight.*

He entered a very plush room, but the opulent décor could not hold a candle to the beauty before him. The Princess stood there dressed in a silken robe and silver slippers. Her flaming red hair fell to her shoulders where it curled in toward her neck. Her skin was remarkably clear for a redhead, and bright green eyes flecked with gray showed a kindness blunted by the rigors of her captivity. She was not tall, but Josh estimated she would be about his height back in the real world. He was now convinced he was in some kind of computer game, living out the part as an avatar, but he'd decided to make the most of the experience. He bowed to the Princess. "It's an honor to meet you, your highness."

"Come in and sit down," she said. She seemed very nervous, and her expression was more shock than anything else. She indicated a divan next to a low table holding a silver coffee service on a tray. She turned to her maid. "Gerda, play some music for us, please."

"Yes, ma'am."

Josh hadn't noticed the maid before now. He was much too busy taking in the stunning beauty of the Princess to do that. The maid was a sharp contrast to her mistress. The old crone was heavily wrinkled and a bit stooped with age. Her hair was silver with only a hint of its previous ebony shade. Her clothes were drab and functional. Josh was surprised to see her move very adroitly to a large piano near the door and take a seat at the keyboard. She began to play a very martial air and sang along with the melody in a harsh, quavering voice.

"Can you tell her to play more softly?" Josh asked.

The Princess moved closer to him and whispered, "The room is bugged. I've managed to cover all the cameras I could find, but the microphones are harder to spot. Keep your voice low and her playing will cover our words. It's good to see you, Commander."

"You know me?"

"Yes, of course, you're Commander Josha. I've been aboard your battle cruiser many times. Does your presence here mean I'm to be rescued?"

"Yeah, but I don't know how yet. I think I've got an idea, but I need to talk it over with the rest of my people first."

"How did you manage to get here, and why are you dressed like a Bremen?"

"These pirates think I'm a prospective recruit. I brought some Royal Marines with me. They're dressed like Bremens too, and the pirates think they're going to join up along with me. My ship found a Bremen freighter loaded with food these guys like, and the Captain of that ship agreed to help us out. He's done business with the pirate King before, and he could get us into the stronghold easier. He's negotiating with Sorbius now."

"What can I do to help?"

"I don't know. Nothing, I guess. Just be ready when things start happening."

"They say they'll kill me if our forces attack."

"We won't let that happen. I'll be sure you're safe before we start anything."

"Oh, Commander, I'd kiss you, but I wouldn't want to blow your cover. Just to be in character, I'm going to slap your face now and act like you insulted me. Run for the door as soon as I do that and duck."

"Duck?"

"They're used to me throwing things at anyone who comes in. Ready?"

"Yeah, I guess so."

The slap was real, and Josh felt his face burn as he ran to the door. He remembered to duck just as the silver coffee pot smashed into the door where his head would have been. *She's got a good arm.*

He was glad to see the door open just enough for him to escape, and he ran in a crouch through the space just as the cream pitcher followed the coffee pot. The guard closed the door quickly and stood there smiling. "What'd you say to her?"

"I just told her she was really hot, and I'd like to hang out with her."

Magran reacted with surprise. "Hot? You mean the room was too hot?"

"No, I mean she's a real babe, a looker."

Both men looked at Josh as if he were speaking a strange language.

"Oh, I, ah, ah. It's a Bremen expression. Say, that's a pretty plush apartment for a prison cell."

"That's the King's apartment. He figured she'd feel more comfortable there than in a cell. He prefers his palace in town except when we have to hole-up and fight," Magran said

Magran returned Josh's laser pistol. "Good thing you didn't have this with you. You'd be toast by now. Let's go to lunch. Sorbius always puts on a big feed for any prospective recruits."

CHAPTER 5

The pair returned to the King's palace and entered a spacious hall. Large windows on one side let in the tropical sunlight, flooding the room with a golden glow. A fresh sea breeze blew in, negating the need for air conditioning. Several tables along the opposite wall held food platters, wine decanters and flowers in golden vases. Exotic dancers gyrated on the marble dance floor, and Josh recognized Rollus and the marines seated on either side of Sorbius. Pirate captains sat among his crew, and Josh suspected they were as much for security as for convincing them to join the band. Sorbius rose from his seat and clapped for the music to stop. The dancing girls fell to the floor in obeisance, and the King spoke, "Well, everyone's here now including our little Bremen. Come sit and eat."

The meal was sumptuous and the entertainment lavish and exotic. When the last performer bowed and exited, Sorbius turned to the marines. "Well, now that you know how we live, are you ready to join up?"

Josh spoke up before Lieutenant Rodgers could respond. "Our group elected me to speak for them, and they want to have a conference first, your Majesty."

"Fine, you can use my conference room," Sorbius said.

Hmmm, it's probably bugged just like the princess's room. Better do this outside. Rodgers beat him to it.

"I think I'd like to meet outside in the fresh air. It's such a lovely day."

"No problem. Go right ahead," Sorbius said.

"Captain Rollus, would you please join us?" Josh asked.

"Certainly, if Your Majesty will excuse me?"

"Go, go." Sorbius flicked his hand at the Captain to emphasize the order.

Josh led the group out to a small garden area. They gathered around Josh, but Rollus cautioned them. "Easy, we don't want these guys to realize we're that organized. Break it up."

The men scattered about the garden but still within earshot of each other. Josh spoke first. "The Princess is in the fortress, but she's not heavily guarded. Magran told me there's no more than twenty men on duty there now. One pirate guards her room, and there's two more in the control center. I saw seven in the dorm, so there could be ten more on duty somewhere else inside. There's a tunnel in the back of the building for bringing in supplies, and we could use that to get in, but we'll have to think up some kind of scam to do it. They keep an eye on it all time, and they can blow it up if they have to. What did you guys find out?"

One of the marines spoke up. "I know that tunnel, sir."

Rodgers broke in. "Drop the formal stuff in case this area's bugged."

"Sorry, sir, er I mean Mike." He continued, "The tunnel comes out near one of the native villages. A pirate took me there to see the big temple where the natives worship their god Mulu. He says the rites are something to see. They dance, have a first class feast and load up the altar with all kinds of gifts for Mulu."

"Is that end of the tunnel closed?" Rodgers asked.

"I don't know?" the marine said.

"I do," another marine spoke.

"Go ahead, Villa," Rodgers said.

"My escort showed me the gate. It's locked, but the control center'll open it up if the natives are bringin' in food or if one of their guys needs to get in to escape from the native rebels."

Another Marine stood. "Yeah, they got a small group of natives living in the jungle who make trouble for them every now and then. My guy said they've tried to wipe 'em out, but the jungle's too thick. He said they set ambushes at night, kill a few pirates then melt into the underbrush. He thinks they've got spider holes all over the place and tunnels to hide in during the day."

"When's the next big party supposed to happen?" Josh asked.

"He said just before sunset tonight," a marine answered.

Josh consulted his watch. "That's six hours from now. We should have plenty of time. Here's my plan. Rollus, have you made a deal with Sorbius yet?"

"Yes, but I wanted to talk to you before I left," Rollus said.

"Good, go back to your ship and load the marines. Come back here as soon as you can. In the meantime, we'll find some way to get inside the fortress using the tunnel."

"I'll need a code word to let me know you've succeeded," Rollus said.

Hmmm, how does that marine song go? From the hall of Montezuma... That's it.

"We'll use the word 'Montezuma'," Josh said.

"What is Montezuma?" Rollus asked.

"It's ah...it's something to do with marines," Josh said.

"Never heard of any Montezuma," Rodgers said.

"Oh well, it's as good as anything," Rollus said. "Montezuma it is. I'll go back to Sorbius now and say my goodbyes, if that's okay with you."

"Sure, go ahead," Josh said, and Rollus left the group.

"How do you plan to get us in the tunnel?" Rodgers asked.

"I'll talk to the native chief. Maybe he'll agree to stage a phony attack."

"Sounds good," Rodgers said. "But, what if the natives won't go along with the deal?"

"I don't see why they wouldn't. After all, we're freeing them from the pirates," Josh said.

"All we got are laser pistols. What about some real weapons?" a Marine asked.

"There's all kinds of stuff in the fortress arsenal, once we get inside," Josh said.

"Okay, it's all planned. Now, we need you to tell Sorbius about the native ritual so we can attend it," Rodgers said to Josh.

"I can do that," Josh said.

"He'll probably want to send some pirates with us," a Marine said.

"As long as there's not too many, we can take 'em, can't we?" Rodgers said. The Marines responded with a rousing, "Yes, sir."

"Keep it down, guys," Josh said. "Don't blow our cover now."

"What do we say to Sorbius now? He expects us to have made our decision about joining the pirates," Rodgers said.

"I'll tell him we decided to sleep on it. I don't think he'll mind," Josh said.

The group returned to Sorbius.

As they entered, the king was enjoying the performance of a very inventive juggler. Sorbius dismissed him and turned to the Marines. "Are you with us?"

"We've still got a few hold-outs," Josh said. "They want to sleep on it, and the rest of us want to see the big native ritual anyway."

"Fine, fine, it's well worth seeing. I'll have a skimmer bus take you to the village just before dusk. You men can relax in my palace until then."

CHAPTER 6

The skimmer bus arrived late that afternoon, and Josh and the marines boarded it along with two heavily armed pirates and the driver.

"Why all the heavy artillery?" Rodgers asked one of the pirates.

"We have to go through territory controlled by the native rebels. They usually don't attack a bus, but there's always a first time," the pirate responded.

Josh was enjoying the jungle scenery on either side of the road when a loud crash caused him to look ahead. A large tree lay across the road, and the bus came to a stop just short of it.

"Look out for trouble," one of the pirates yelled as he raised a window and aimed his laser rifle at the jungle. The other pirate did the same on the other side.

"Hit the floor," Rodgers called, and the marines left their seats for the aisle way. Josh followed suit.

A loud speaker in the jungle called out, "All we want are your weapons and money. Throw out your weapons and come out with your hands up, and nobody gets hurt."

A pirate yelled back, "Yeah, yeah, and pigs fly. Come and get 'em."

"I'm serious. This is Kanigi, and I give you my word on it."

The other pirate spoke, "Hey, I've heard this Kanigi guy's as good as his word. Why not do as he says?"

Josh had a thought. *Hey, this guy may be able to help us.* He spoke to the pirate who seemed to be in charge, "Let me talk to him a minute. I may be able to convince him to back off."

"Be my guest. It's your funeral," the pirate said.

Josh handed his laser pistol to the pirate and walked out of the bus with his hands up. He called into the jungle, "Hey, can we talk a minute?"

"Walk straight ahead until you can't see the bus anymore," the voice answered.

Josh complied and soon found himself surrounded by lush, green growth. He continued on until a voice behind him spoke.

"That's far enough. Turn around."

Josh turned to face a large native pointing a laser rifle at his stomach. Like all the natives his hair was coal black and frizzed into a large ball surrounding his head. His bronze complexion contrasted with the red sarong folded neatly around his waist and the string of pink shells around his neck. Perspiration highlighted his well-defined muscle structure. He was typical of all the native men except for the modern laser rifle and the bandolier of energy packs across his chest.

"Are you Kanigi?" Josh asked.

"Yeah. Did you guys decide to join the pirates?"

"Not yet, we need to talk to your chief first, but how did you know about us?" Josh said.

"Hey, it's an island—hard to keep a secret around here. Besides, we make it a point to know everything that goes on in the pirate's palace and fortress."

"Who's we?" Josh said.

"I'm sure they've told you about the native rebels. We call ourselves the Wagona, it's a native term that means something like 'freedom fighter' in your language. I can take you to the chief and translate for you. He doesn't speak any language but our native tongue. What do you want with him?"

Josh leaned closer to the native and lowered his voice. "We aren't pirates, we're Royal Truvian Marines, and we're here to rescue the princess they captured. Once she's safe, my ship will return and wipe out the pirates. I'll need your chief's help to stage a scene so that we can get into the fortress through the tunnel. Once inside, we'll get the princess and call in our ship."

Kanigi threw back his head in laughter, and his band joined him. "You've got to be kidding. There's only nine of you, I counted."

"Six, the other three are real pirates. Anyway, we've got more coming and a Battle Cruiser to back them up. All we need is some help fooling the pirates in the fortress so they'll let us in. There aren't that many on duty there now," Josh said.

"There's enough to take care of six Marines," Kanigi said.

"Here's the deal. They think we're ready to join up with them, so they aren't suspicious yet. We need you guys to be offended, or something, and attack us. We fall back on the tunnel entrance and call for help. The fortress lets us into the tunnel, and we go in and take out the guys there while we make sure the Princess is safe. The rest of the Marines land in the city and take out the pirates there while the ship handles the orbital station and any pirate ships they have nearby. We take the Princess up to the ship, then we bug out for home."

"Not a bad idea, but I don't think the Chief'll go for it."

"Why not?" Josh asked.

"He's on the pirate's payroll, and he's not about to kill the goose that lays the golden eggs. Besides, you don't need him when you've got us."

"How's that?"

"We can pretend to attack you, and we're a lot more credible where the pirates are concerned. Just let us into the fortress also, so we can get hold of the weapons there, and it's a deal."

"What about the pirates on the bus?"

"If you can get 'em to come off unarmed, we'll take care of them."

"Okay, I'll go back and try to talk 'em into surrendering."

"Good, just turn around and walk back the way you came. I'll be waiting to see them come off the bus."

Kanigi melted back into the bush, and Josh began retracing his steps. He soon spotted the bus. Once aboard, he spoke to the head pirate. "I think we can trust this guy. He says we can go back right away if we give him our guns and gold, and I think he's sincere."

"See, I told ya," the other pirate said. "This stuff isn't worth gettin' killed for." He patted his laser rifle.

"Yeah, I got a wife and kids back in the city," the bus driver added.

"Okay, okay, we'll give up," the pirate said. He turned to the marines, "Look, we all go out carrying our weapons like this." He unstrapped his laser pistol and slung it over one arm. Then, he placed his rifle over his outstretched arms and walked to the door. "Okay, we're commin' out," he yelled toward the jungle.

As the passengers and driver emerged from the bus, armed natives materialized from the jungle all around them. Kanigi gave orders in the native language, and the pirates were soon whisked away into the brush. He moved to Josh.

"Okay, they'll be on ice until later. Do you want their weapons?"

"Yes, we'd like to have them," Rodgers said.

As the rest of the marines re-fastened their laser pistols around their waists, Rodgers instructed two of them to pick up the pirate's weapons. When they were ready to go, Kanigi led them toward the tunnel entrance. On the way he briefed Josh and Rodgers.

"When we get close I'll tell you to start shooting into the jungle. Make sure you aim high. We'll shoot back, being sure not to hit you. You'll need the code to open the door. Did they give it to you?"

"Code? What code?" Rodgers asked.

"There's a keypad on the door. It takes a four digit code to open it. All the pirates know it. I'm surprised they didn't give it to you."

"The only code I saw anyone use was on the princess's door. I guess we could try that one," Josh said.

"If that doesn't work, you'll just have to try to talk your way in. We won't be able to help you right away. They'll close the tunnel door as soon as you guys are inside. You'll have to get into the control room and open up for us as soon as you can," Kanigi said.

"We'll make that our first priority," Josh said.

"I think we're all set. I'll tell you when we need to start the fireworks," Kanigi said.

CHAPTER 7

Kanigi led them down a path to an apparent dead end then pointed to a small sapling. "Pull up on that sapling and the opening will appear. I'm going to move out of sight. The pirates have a camera covering this area, and they only turn it on if that tree's moved. We'll start shooting now. You run to the sapling and start shooting back before you pull it. We'll keep shooting until you're inside. Good luck." He melted into the jungle, and laser blasts began to hit around the tunnel gate area. Josh and the marines fell back to the entrance and began returning fire.

A strong pull on the slender trunk produced a growling sound as a section of foliage slid away from an iron gate. Josh tried the princess's door code on the keypad, but nothing happened. A voice spoke from above the door, "Oh, it's you guys. Who told you about the entrance?"

"Never mind about that now. Open up quick. We're being attacked by the rebels. They ambushed the bus, but we managed to make it here. Open up," Josh said.

"Gordus knows the code, he can open it."

"Gordus is dead. The rebels got him. Open up."

"How about Tully or the driver?"

"Tully led us here and got it just before I pulled on the tree. The last I saw of the driver he was running back along the road as fast as he could go. Open up. We can't hold on much longer with only laser pistols."

"Sorry, I'll send some men to help you out, but I can't open the door without a password." The speaker fell silent, and the foliage closed back.

Josh stood back from the door. *Where is Kanigi when I need him?*

"Psst, over here." A voice from the jungle summoned Josh to the edge of the bush.

"That you, Kanigi?"

"Yeah, go into the jungle."

Josh pushed into the bush and soon found a small clearing where Kanigi and his men surrounded three very frightened pirates.

"Good work," Josh said. "Any of them ready to tell us the code?"

"You try 'em first," Kanigi said.

Josh moved to the one doing the most shaking. "Okay, what's the code?"

"I can't tell you. They'd kill me if I did," the pirate answered.

Josh noticed Kanigi was testing the edge of a large knife. "That might be better than what these guys have in store for you. Which way do you want to go? You can watch while they work on your buddies. Maybe one of them'll break first."

"Oh god, tell him now. We won't squeal on you, Ben," another pirate said.

"Okay, okay, it's 8127," the first pirate said.

Once more Josh moved back to his men and pulled on the sapling. The bushes moved away again, and he entered 8127.

"Hey, I thought you didn't know the code."

Tully told one of my guys before he croaked.

The door slid back and the Marines hurried inside. The door closed behind them, and Josh led them to the fortress entrance. As that door opened, Josh saw a small group of armed pirates waiting. He counted seven pirates which meant there were some 13 to be accounted for later. He knew two were in the control room and one was guarding the Princess—that left ten somewhere else in the fortress. He calculated that at least five would be in the barracks area off duty, meaning five were on duty elsewhere. He noticed the pirates relaxing visibly now that the tunnel door was secure and no natives were inside the tunnel. He quickly pulled his laser pistol and shoved it into the back of the closest pirate. The Marines saw his move and subdued the remaining brigands.

"Okay, keep quiet and nobody gets hurt," Josh said. *Jeez, how corny can you get, but it's all I could think of.*

"What's this all about?" one of the pirates asked.

Lieutenant Rodgers took over. "You're all now prisoners of the Truvian Royal Marines. Drop your weapons." The pirates complied, and Bowers herded them into one corner of the entryway while two Marines picked up the weapons and distributed the automatic rifles and ammunition bandoliers to the rest of the group. "Where to now, Commander?" Rodgers asked.

"This way." Josh led his men to the barracks area where the off duty pirates were easily subdued. He could now account for sixteen pirates, but his squad was down to five men to face whatever remained of the fortress garrison. He turned to Rodgers. "We have to get to the control center and open up the tunnel for Kanigi's men before we rescue the Princess. We're not in any position to stave off a counter attack."

"Right, lead the way," Rodgers agreed.

The men in the control center were just as surprised, but one of them managed to push an alarm button before a Marine knocked him cold with the butt of his rifle. A claxon began to sound a glaring noise. Josh moved to the console and studied the controls. They were labeled in Diluran. He turned to his men. "Anybody able to read this stuff?"

One Marine stepped forward. "I can't, but he can." He grasped the pirate's neck with both hands, and the man's expression went blank. "He'll do what you tell him now, Commander."

"What was that?" Josh asked.

"It's a Gordian hypnohold, but I can't hold it very long, sir."

Josh spoke to the pirate, shouting over the noise. "Open both ends of the tunnel."

"Cant do that. Only open one door at a time."

"Then open the outer door now."

The pirated touched a button area, and his display showed the symbol of an open door with Diluran text below the icon.

"I think he did it," one of the marines yelled as he pointed to a video screen showing armed native men rushing down a hallway.

"Great. Now open the inner door," Josh yelled.

The pirate complied, and the Marine released his grip. The pirate slumped over his console unconscious.

"This way to the Princess," Josh yelled.

As they ran out of the control room, they encountered gunfire from an intersecting hallway. "Keep their heads down, Rodgers," Josh shouted. "I'll make a run for the Princess's room."

"You got it commander," Rodgers replied. The Marines poured a steady fire at the hallway, and Josh ran to the stairway leading to the Princess's room. The claxon still sounded almost drowning out his own thoughts, but his communicator came alive just as he reached the next floor.

"Commander, we're ready to dock at the orbiting station. Is the Princess safe?" It was Rollus's voice.

"I'll know that in a minute, but go ahead and dock we need all the help we can get. We've set off the alarm at the fortress, and I imagine the pirates in the town'll be here any minute."

"I understand. We're going in now."

Josh peered around a corner and saw the guard moving toward the door to the Princess's room. He stepped into view and leveled his laser pistol at the pirate.

"Hold it there," Josh called.

The pirate froze and raised his hands in the air. "Take it easy. I was going to let her out. She'll be dead in five minutes if I don't, but the keypad's all screwed up."

Josh ran to the door and now understood the pirate's problem. The keypad blinked red for all numbers.

"Commander to Rodgers, come in please." Josh called.

"This is Rodgers, sir. Go ahead."

"The keypad on the Princess's door is flashing red all over. The alarm must have neutralized it. You'll have to turn off the alarm."

"We're pretty busy right now, sir. The rest of the garrison's got us pinned down here. We need some help ourselves."

"My guys are on the way."

Josh turned to see Kanigi behind him. "Glad you're here. We need to get to the control room so we can reactivate the keypad lock on the Princess's door."

"Wait a bit. We should have the fortress cleared out in a few minutes."

The claxon noise stopped, and a voice from inside the room said, "What's going on?"

Josh moved to the door and slid back the peep hole. The confident royal eyes he'd seen before now showed a hint of fear, and she held a dainty lace handkerchief over her nose and mouth.

"Am I glad to see you. Can you open the door?" the Princess said.

"I can't, the keypad's all screwed up, and we have to go to the control room to see if we can straighten it out."

"You'd better hurry. There's some kind of gas coming out of one of the air vents in here," the Princess said.

"That's what I was tellin' you about," the pirate guard said.

Out of instinct Josh grasped the door handle. To his surprise it flew open. The Princess ran out followed closely by her maid. Josh slammed the door closed behind them.

"Why did we rescue this one?" Kanigi said, pointing to the maid.

The Princess ran to Kanigi and began beating on his bare chest. "You dirty savage, she's my maid, and she's done more for me than you ever will."

"Easy, your highness, Kanigi here's the reason you're still alive. If it wasn't for his help, you'd still be throwing things at the peep hole," Josh said.

She stepped back and softened her expression. "I'm sorry. Thank you for your help."

"No problem, lady."

Josh's communicator came alive. "This is Rollus, we've got the orbital station, and more marines are on their way. Looks like you're going to need them. A lot of pirates are heading out of the city to take back the fortress."

"Got it. Where's the Ares?" Josh said.

"She's busy with the pirate ships, but all the marines are with me. I'm sending them down as fast as I can. Major Burns says he'll attack the pirates from the rear as soon as all his men are down. Can you hold the fortress?"

"I think we can," Josh said. "Talk to you later."

"We'd better get out of here," Kanigi said, pointing to the gas beginning to ooze under the door.

"How many men did you get in?" he asked Kanigi.

"We got thirty in before they closed the outer door."

"Okay, let's get to the control room and set up the defense. Those pirates'll be here any minute now."

"What about him?" Kanigi pointed to the pirate guard.

"Hey, I don't want no trouble. Just let me get outa here so's I can get back home. This pirate stuff's for the birds."

"Go down to the barracks area and wait there," Josh said.

"Yes, sir." The pirate bounded down the steps and out of sight.

The group moved to the control room where Rodgers was busy issuing orders. He called the room to attention as Josh and the Princess walked in.

"At ease," Josh said. *I think that's what I'm supposed to say.* The men relaxed, and Bowers found a chair for the Princess and her maid. "What's up?" Josh said.

"The natives are guarding the prisoners. We've herded them all into the barracks. We have one wounded, that's all.

We had to kill two of the pirates. Your natives lost three, Kanigi. I'm sorry," Rodgers said.

"They were all volunteers," Kanigi said.

"My men are manning the heavy weapons, and the natives are on the rifle ports. I've got Bowers, here, on the console in case of an air attack. He's managed to figure out the controls," Rodgers continued.

Josh's communicator came on. "Jordan to Rodgers."

"Go ahead, this is Rodgers."

"The pirates are here, and they brought some heavy stuff with 'em. We got anything that'll take out artillery?"

Rodgers turned to Bowers who was busy scanning the control panel. "Any luck?"

"I think these missiles might do it, but they'd need a laser designator on the target."

Just then a loud boom rocked the fortress. "I guess they've got our range now," Rodgers said.

Josh called back to Jordan, "Jordan, this is the Commander. I can't believe these pirates don't have some sort of laser designator handy."

"I looked around, sir, and I can't find any."

Josh turned to Rodgers. "Send somebody down to the armory. There must be one there."

"Yes, sir," Rodgers responded. "Rogers to Simpson."

"This is Simpson, sir."

"You're our weapons expert. Checkout the armory for a designator."

"Yes, sir, on my way now."

Another shot rocked the building as Bowers pointed to a screen. "The pirates are trying to get into the tunnel, sir."

"Don't you control the outer door?" Josh asked him.

"Looks like they've set some sort of explosive charge to blow it open. They're all moving away from it now."

"Blow the tunnel," Josh commanded.

Bowers scanned the console for the right button, but another boom from farther away indicated the pirates had blown the tunnel door.

Rodgers pointed to another screen. "They're in the tunnel now."

"Blow it, blow it," Josh yelled.

Bowers pushed two buttons with no results except the sound of a missile launching from the roof. Josh moved to the console trying to remember which button the pirate showed him earlier. "I think it's this one," he said as he pushed it. The screen showing the tunnel went dark.

"You got it, Commander," Rodgers yelled.

Another artillery shot rocked the fortress, and Josh felt the Princess's hand on his arm.

"Are we going to be all right?" she asked.

He looked into those wonderful eyes trying to hold back tears, and his heart melted.

"Don't worry, your highness. The rest of the marines will be here soon, and it'll all be over before you know it," Josh said.

Another shot caused sparks to fly from the console and flames to dart from a wall panel. Rodgers grabbed a fire extinguisher and doused the flames as Bowers announced the loss of his outside cameras.

"Blake to Commander, Blake to Commander." Josh's ear bud called.

"Go ahead, this is the Commander."

"The last of our marines are on the surface now. A few of the crew also volunteered to help out. They're on their way now."

"That's good news, but be careful, the pirates have some heavy artillery. They're pounding us pretty hard. Anything the ship can do?"

"Our missiles are too powerful. If we hit the pirates, we'll also rock you pretty hard."

"I think we can hold out. The walls are pretty thick."

"Commander, Commander, I got a designator, and I've got it locked on the big gun. You can fire any time."

"Got it," Bowers called. He pushed a button, and the sound of a missile launching cut off the next artillery shock. It was the last one as a chorus of cheers from the marines manning the walls told Josh the shot was a success.

"Who fired that anti-spaceship missile?" Blake's voice dampened the gaiety.

"Sorry, it was an accident," Josh responded.

"Darn near hit us. Lucky our sensors spotted it in time."

"We just got the artillery piece with one of our missiles. Just waiting for the rest of the marines to attack."

"We've got the pirate's space ships on the run with only minor damage. Destroyed five, but four got away."

"Good work. Once we get this place secure, I'll bring the Princess up to the Ares."

"We'll be waiting. Over and out."

More cheers accompanied by heavier gunfire signaled the arrival of the rest of the marines.

"Major Burns to Commander."

"Go ahead, Burns."

"The pirates have surrendered. There weren't that many left when we showed up. The natives have been harassing them pretty heavily, and none of them wanted to be left to their tender mercies."

Josh turned to the Princess. "Looks like you're headed back home."

CHAPTER 8

"How can I ever thank you?" Ariadne said. "Your thanks should go to the marines, but most of all, to Kanigi and his men. We couldn't have done it without them."

Ariadne moved to Kanigi and embraced him. "Thank you, too. Your people are now free of the pirates."

"For a while, lady, but they'll be back once these men are gone." He gestured toward the marines in the control room.

"My marines will train you on the weapons in this fortress," Josh said. "And, the Ares will stay in orbit to take care of any pirate ships thinking they can take up where they left off."

At that point Major Burns entered the control room. "We've got a ton of prisoners, Commander. They won't all fit in the Ares brig. What should we do with them?"

"We can solve that problem for you," Kanigi said.

I imagine they can, but even though they're pirates, it wouldn't be humane to let the natives torture them. "Does Rollus have any room in his holds for them?" Josh asked.

"I thought of that, but he says his ship's fully loaded, and he has to get on to Rigna II before he runs out of coolant for the frozen stuff."

Hmmm, I wonder if any of the pirate ships are salvageable. Josh called the ship. "Blake, we need a prison ship. Any of the pirate ships fixable?"

"We captured one almost intact. The crew surrendered and

we've got a prize crew aboard guarding them."

"How many pirates here?" Josh asked Burns.

"I'd say about 150. We did have around 200, but the natives spirited off a lot of them before we could set up a perimeter."

"Blake, could you handle 150 more?" Josh called.

"It'd be tight quarters for the pirates, and we'd need a lot more guards, but we could take them to the penal colony on Hagon, that's only three days away."

"How soon could the captured pirate ship be ready?"

"Give us 24 hours."

Josh looked at Burns. "Can you manage to keep the pirates under control that long?"

"Yes, sir. I'll have the Ares send down some laser fence, and we can set up a prison camp around some houses a couple of miles down the road."

"Okay, get it set up. Rodgers can start weapons classes for the natives in the morning. You know who you need for that, Rodgers?"

"Yes, sir. With Major Burns' permission I'll pick my men."

"Go ahead, Rodgers," Burns said.

A marine entered the control center and saluted Josh.

Oh yeah, that's what these guys do. Let's see, I think it goes like this. Josh formed his best imitation of a salute, but he noticed marines stifling laughter.

"Sir, there's a native outside looking for you. He only speaks the native tongue, but he looks important. Shall I let him in?"

"That'd be our Chief," Kanigi said.

"Sure, bring him up here so Kanigi can translate."

"Yes, sir." The marine saluted, showing the professional

training he'd received, and Josh returned it as best he could.

In a few moments the Chief appeared with an entourage of sub-chiefs and the Shaman. He spoke to Kanigi.

"The Chief says there'll be a big party tonight in the village, and he wants all of us to attend. He says he's got a special honor for you, Commander."

"Well, how can we say no. What time?"

"He says sunset tonight," Kanigi translated.

"Tell him we'll be there," Josh said.

The Chief moved to Josh and embraced him, kissing him on both cheeks. Josh recoiled a bit but noticed Kanigi shaking his head vigorously and returned the embrace without the kisses.

The Chief and his party left, and Josh consulted Burns. "Can you have your prison camp set up by then?"

"No problem. I wouldn't want to miss the party," Burns said.

Things were calming down all over the island now, and Josh turned to Ariadne. "You can get your things together and get ready to leave for the ship, if you like."

"I don't think the quarters on the ship will be nearly as nice as the room they held me captive in," she said. "If the gas has cleared out, I'd like to go back there."

"We'll check it out." Josh sent a marine to find a gas test kit and clear the Princess's old room.

"Shall I ask the ship to send down some tents for my men?" Burns asked.

"They can use the old pirate barracks. They also have a mess hall in the fortress, if any of your people can cook," Josh said.

"No problem, we'll move in here," Burns said.

"What will you do until the party, Commander?" Ariadne asked Josh.

"I guess I'll need to clean up a little and put on a uniform. I'll go back to the Ares and do that."

"Why don't you just have them send down a uniform? You can clean up in my quarters," she said.

Oh boy, how do you turn that invitation down? "Good idea, your highness." He called the ship to send a uniform and followed the Princess and her maid to the old room.

A marine in a haz-mat suit stood outside with a small unit in his hand. Lights blinked on and off as he scanned it across the entryway. He turned when he heard the footsteps behind him and pulled off the hood. "It's okay, sir. No trace of any gas now. The ventilation system must have pulled it all out of here."

"Thanks, the Princess was eager to get back," Josh said.

"She can have it now," the marine said as he headed for the stairway.

"Come in and get comfortable, Commander. We have plenty of time until the ceremony," the Princess said.

She led Josh into the plush room he'd seen before and plopped down on a divan. She patted the cushion next to her. "Sit here with me. Your uniform won't be here for a while."

Josh took the seat as the Princess ordered her maid. "Bring us a glass of that good white wine, please Gerda."

"Yes, m'lady," Gerda said as she moved to a cabinet in one wall. She soon returned with two glasses on a silver tray. The Princess took one glass, and Gerda held the tray for Josh.

My parents don't let me have beer yet. I've never tasted wine, but there's a first time for everything. Hey, this stuff's not bad. I was expecting something sweeter, but I kinda like it.

Ariadne moved closer to Josh. Her perfume was muted now, but the mixture of her perspiration and the remnant of her cologne produced an intoxicating sensation greater than the wine.

"You know, I've always admired you, Commander. Even when I was a little girl aboard your ship with my parents, and you were only a junior officer taking orders instead of giving them, I thought you were marvelous."

"You did?" Josh's voice broke a bit at this disclosure.

"Then I grew up, and you were more senior in rank, I used to fantasize about you and I alone on some remote planet falling in love."

Josh edged a bit away from her to the end of the divan. "Your Highness, I don't think your father would approve of you having fantasies about a Space Force officer."

"I don't care what he thinks. Here we are together on some remote planet, just like in my dreams. Make my dreams come true." She pressed her lips to his, and his heart raced.

I've never done a video game like this. What am I supposed to do? I can't do what she wants me to do. This must be some kind of test in this game. If I give in, someone'll come through that door and kill me for making love to a Princess, I'm sure of that. I gotta get out of this some way. He broke off the kiss and stood up, dropping the Princess face first on the divan.

"I'm sorry, Your Highness, I can't do this. I'd never be able to face your father again if I did."

"I told you, I don't care about Father. Come back here." She sat up and held her arms out toward him.

There must be some kind of vow this guy took to be an officer. It had to have something to do with loyalty to the king. "I took an oath to be loyal to the King. I don't think that includes making love to his daughter."

"I could give you a royal order to kiss me again. Would you obey that?"

"Look, you're a beautiful lady, and I'd love to kiss you all day, but it goes against all my conscience to do that. Please don't make this difficult for me."

The Princess's mood turned sour. She picked up her wine glass and threw it at the door just as a junior officer from the Ares was opening it up. He ducked back outside just in time. After the impact, he poked a tentative head around the door.

"Is this a bad time, sir? I can come back later," he said.

"No, no, come on in," Josh called. *Thank God, I'm saved.*

The Lieutenant entered carrying a hang-up bag. "I brought your dress uniform, sir. The XO said it was an important occasion."

"Thank you, ah, I can't place your name," Josh said.

"Norton, sir, Lieutenant Brad Norton."

"Thank you, Lieutenant Norton. You may return to the ship now."

"Yes, sir." He leaned closer to Josh and whispered, "I hope the rest of the afternoon goes better for you."

"You may leave now, Lieutenant," Josh almost shouted.

The young man moved quickly out the door and Josh turned to see Ariadne fuming on the divan. "You might as well clean up and go back to your ship, Commander. I think we're finished here."

"Yes, Your Highness." Josh followed Gerda into a very lavish bathroom and hung his bag on a convenient hook.

"The shower is there," Gerda pointed to a sunken area with

a circular curtain rod and an overhead array of nozzles. "You'll figure out how the controls work in no time."

She left him alone to fiddle with the knobs and levers and enjoy the different spray patterns while he showered. He found an electric razor and some manly colognes before dressing in the fancy uniform. It even included a tall hat with a fancy feather on top. He walked back out into the sitting area, but no one was there. He took the hint and went down to the control room. Kanigi was waiting for him along with Blake and some other officers from the Ares. They all smiled knowingly as he entered.

Blake spoke. "Did you and the Princess have a good *talk?*"

The other men stifled laughter and took on sober expressions after a cold stare from Josh.

"We did—a very *proper* talk, I might add. She's getting ready for the ceremony tonight." Josh said.

Kanigi moved to Josh and fingered his dress uniform. "You guys clean up pretty good. I love the hat." He stroked the ostrich plumes almost affectionately.

"I'm hungry. Anything to eat?" Josh said. *That's funny, I'm not hungry, but he is.*

"I was just going to mention dinner. Kanigi's people brought in some kind of native fish, and he translated cooking instructions for our guys in the kitchen. It should be ready by now," Blake said.

"Then let's go," Josh said.

CHAPTER 9

Josh and his officers arrived at the ceremonial clearing accompanied by Kanigi who would act as their interpreter. Princess Ariadne was already seated on a special throne next to the Chief. A warrior spoke to Kanigi, and he translated. "Would all of you please sit in this area except for the Commander."

"Where do I go?" Josh asked.

Kanigi consulted the warrior and indicated an empty chair next to the Princess. "The Chief wants you there."

"Stay close in case I need help," Josh said.

"I'll be right behind you," Kanigi said.

When everyone was seated the Chief stood and gave a command in the native language. He resumed his seat, and the drums began a lively beat. A dozen native women in their long palm skirts and bikini tops moved into the clearing and began a sensual dance.

A voice from behind said, "Ever see anything like that?"

It was Kanigi, and Josh responded, "Only on TV."

"What's TV?" Kanigi said.

"It's like a small movie in a box," Josh said.

"Whatever." Kanigi shrugged his shoulders in resignation, considering further discussion pointless.

The dancers finished their performance by dropping to their knees and bowing to the Chief. He waved a hand, and the ladies made a quick exit. The drums changed to a more warlike beat, and several warriors wielding large clubs studded with what Josh guessed were shark teeth. They scanned the area as if watching for attackers and danced in a deliberate manner while grunting guttural challenges.

In response to their calls several high-pitched warbles came from the nearby bush. The dancers stopped and backed into a defensive formation as the same number of men appeared out of the bush dressed like pirates and carrying laser rifles. They danced to a point opposite the native warriors and began a dance simulating a rifle attack.

The native warriors then danced into close contact with the pseudo-pirates and the group began to gyrate in a manner imitating hand-to-hand combat. One by one, the natives defeated the "pirates", and the "dead" pirates ran off into the bush. When all the "pirates" were defeated, the natives danced in celebration and ran off into the bush after the "pirates".

The drums took on a somber beat, and a monotone chant from the bush signaled a grisly procession back into the clearing. Each of the native warriors had exchanged their war clubs for a stake holding a coconut carved to resemble the severed head of a pirate. They paraded past the Chief who beamed his pleasure at the display, but the Princess had to fight back the urge to vomit at the sight.

They finished their procession around the clearing to the cheers of the other natives and planted their trophies in a line of holes before the statue of Mulu. They too then dropped to one knee and bowed to the Chief before departing to be replaced by the Shaman and his acolytes.

The Chief rose and made an announcement then turned to Josh and spoke.

"That's your cue," Kanigi whispered.

"What do I do?" Josh said.

"You walk to the Shaman and make a bit of a bow—nothing too low, but enough to show respect. I'll be right behind you."

Josh rose and walked to the Shaman accompanied by applause from the natives. The drums resumed a somber beat, and the Shaman wailed a long diatribe.

"What's he saying?" Josh asked Kanigi.

"He's telling about how many pirates you killed."

"I didn't kill anybody," Josh protested.

"Hey, don't be modest. You get credit for all the casualties, because you were in charge. It's an old tribal custom."

One of the acolytes stepped forward and handed the Shaman a bamboo box. The Shaman took it and moved toward Josh intoning some sort of prayer.

"What now?" Josh asked.

"He's going to present you with your Mahiki."

"What's that?"

"The Chief's going to make you a Sagata. The Mahiki tells everyone you're a Sagata."

"Okay, is this going to hurt?"

"No, it's a thing that goes around your neck."

The Shaman opened the box revealing a small stone image of the god Mulu on a leather thong. Josh hadn't noticed the Chief leaving his throne and joining them until Kanigi whispered, "Bow to the Chief."

Josh turned and bowed as the Chief took the necklace from the Shaman. The drums stopped, and the Shaman began a monotone chant as the Chief tied the leather thong around Josh's neck. When the image was securely fastened, the Chief embraced Josh and kissed him on both cheeks.

"Kiss him back," Kanigi whispered.

Josh returned the Chief's kisses, and the natives erupted into loud cheers. The Chief raised Josh's arm into the air as the drums took up a fast-paced beat. The Chief led Josh back to his chair next to the Princess. She touched his arm and leaned closer to him.

"I'm sorry I put you in an awkward position earlier," she said.

"That's okay, I was really glad you like me, but after all, you're a princess and I'm only a kid."

The Princess laughed. "A kid? Commander, you must be all of 40."

Jeez, I forgot I'm a grown man in this game. "I mean a kid from a poor family."

"Poor? Your family's one of the richest in the kingdom. What's wrong with you? Are you sick, or something? Your blood's as blue as mine. You're descended from a line of kings who ruled Truvia for two hundred years."

"Yeah, I forgot, but that was a long time ago."

"Well, yes, but it doesn't change the fact that I could marry you if I wished, and my father couldn't object on the basis of your bloodline. After rescuing me from the pirates, he'd probably welcome our union."

Oh boy, this gets better and better.

A line of natives bearing gifts interrupted their conversation. Josh leaned closer to Kanigi. "What's this about?"

"It's customary for a village to present gifts to a Sagata who rescues them from disaster. These are all yours." He swept his arm across the parade.

The first gift was a necklace of sea shells, and Josh handed that to the Princess. Next came a feather cape.

"Put it on," Kanigi said.

Josh rose and donned the cape to the applause of the villagers.

The next man presented Josh with a baby pig. "What do I do with this?" Josh asked Kanigi.

"You just kiss it and give it back to him. He'll raise it to maturity and give you the meat."

Josh kissed the pig and thought of how such an act was something to be ridiculed back home, but the natives responded with ooohs and aaaahs.

More jewelry followed plus a long line of women bearing food. "I can't eat all this," Josh said.

"You bless it for the feast," Kanigi prompted.

"How do I do that?"

Kanigi moved closer to Josh and gave him a surreptitious demonstration of the hand motions required. "Like that."

Josh made the movement over each dish as the natives applauded each blessing. Finally, a lovely young native girl prostrated herself at Josh's feet. She couldn't have been more than a teenager, but she was quite lovely.

"Who's this?" Josh asked.

"It's one of the Chief's nieces. She's yours now," he replied.

"What do you mean 'mine'?"

"She's your slave. Oh, you could marry her if you wanted, but you don't have to."

"I don't want a slave."

"Well, you can't turn her down. The Chief'd have to kill her if you rejected her."

"That's barbaric."

"Look around, you see any people here in black tie?" Kanigi chided.

"Go ahead and take her as a slave." The Princess's voice broke in.

"Why?" Josh asked her.

"Darling, she could be one of our servants after we're married."

"Who says we're getting married?"

"I do. I'll have my father order it if you don't propose."

Hey Josh, it's only a silly game. Go along with her. "Sure I'll propose to you. Right after this party."

The Princess plopped back in her chair and rolled her eyes. "How romantic."

"She's still lying there. What do I do?" Josh asked Kanigi.

"Just lift her to her feet and let her sit down next to your chair."

Josh complied as the natives cheered vigorously.

The rest of the evening included entertainment and some delicious food. As they walked back to the fortress, the Princess moved close to Josh. "I'm glad you want to marry me. I don't care about our age difference."

"What about her?" Josh nodded toward the Chief's niece who was still following a few paces behind him.

"She'll be one of my maids. I'll keep her with Gerda and me until we get back home. Maybe I can teach her some of our language on the way."

"Good, I wouldn't trust my crew with her aboard."

CHAPTER 10

Two days later Ariadne called for Josh after breakfast. She was still taking all her meals in her room while Josh was eating with the men in the pirate's old mess hall. Josh knocked on her door, and Gerda opened it after checking through the peep hole to verify the caller.

Ariadne was busy fitting a dress on the Chief's niece, who seemed to be taking the idea of wearing a lot of clothes rather poorly.

"Hold still, Vallana, or I'll stick you with these pins," Ariadne said.

"Does she understand you?" Josh asked.

"Oh, good morning, Commander. No, but she understands I won't let her run around in a sarong with no underwear. Luckily, Gerda found some clothes about her size in one of the city's shops. They just need some tailoring."

"Eeeek," Vallana pulled away and let loose with a volley of the native tongue. She ran to Josh and threw herself at his feet.

"I told you to hold still. It's not my fault you got stuck," Ariadne said.

"At least you found out her name," Josh said.

"That's about all I've been able to do. She keeps asking for her Sagata. That's you, as best I can tell. Maybe you can get through to her."

Josh lifted Vallana to her feet and listened to some soft pleading in her native language. He patted her shoulder in a reassuring manner. "It's okay. The Princess won't hurt you. You have to learn how to wear clothes."

His touch seemed to calm her a bit, but she maintained a vise-like grip on his arm. "Hasn't the ship found some translator software for her language?" Josh asked.

"They say there's none in our data bases. They're checking out some other planets, but haven't had any luck so far."

Josh's face brightened and he snapped his fingers to announce his epiphany. "Say, the pirates had to communicate with them. They must have something."

"Clubs and whips don't need much translation," Ariadne said.

Josh called the Ares. "Blake, this is the Commander."

"Yes, sir—this is Blake."

"I was just thinking, the pirates must have had some way of communicating with the natives. Check them out for some software."

"Good Idea. I'll get Lieutenant Rodgers on it right away. Sorbius is cooperating with us in the hope of some kind of amnesty. We'll try him."

"When you get something, send it to the Princess."

"Will do."

Vallana resumed her pleading, but Josh pushed her back toward Gerda. "Now be a nice girl and let Gerda fit your dress so you can look pretty for me. Okay?" He used gestures and facial expressions to indicate he wanted her to wear the dress, and she seemed to understand. She released her grip and nodded to the maid.

"Thank God," Ariadne said.

"What did you want, your highness?" Josh said.

"Let's take a walk and talk about it." She took up a grip where Vallana left off and steered Josh out to the small garden area behind the fortress. They found a stone bench and sat down.

"Have you heard anything about a relief ship yet?" she asked.

"Nothing, Space Command's trying to round up one, but they claim it'll be a while before they can get anything here."

"I've been bugging Father, but he says he won't interfere in military matters. Really, he makes me so mad. You'd think he didn't care about his daughter getting back for the racing season at Murford Park."

"Is that important?"

"Important! It's only theeeee social event of the year. What's taking your people so long?"

"We can't leave until they have another battle cruiser to replace us. The pirates might try to come back if we weren't here to protect the planet."

Ariadne sighed heavily and pretended to study a large yellow blossom next to the bench. She picked it from its bush and held it to her nose. "What a lovely fragrance."

She held the flower close to Josh's face. "Smell it."

Josh sniffed the bloom and shook his head to clear the smell. "Kinda strong, isn't it?"

"It reminds me of you. Strong, yet sweet." She moved closer and lifted her face to his.

Oh boy, here we go again. I sure wish this wasn't a game. I'd love to kiss her for real. I need some help right now.

"Commander?   Commander?   Are   you   out   here?" Lieutenant Rodgers' voice broke the spell.

"Over here," Josh called.

Rodgers soon spotted them and bowed to the Princess. "Your Highness, the pirates showed us this device they used to communicate with the natives. I brought three units; one for you, one for your maid and one for the girl." He handed the Princess three small ear buds.

"Thank you, Lieutenant," she said as she dropped them into a pocket of her gown.

"I've also got news for you, Commander."

"What is it?"

"Space Command says they can't break loose another battle cruiser to relieve us for a few weeks. Looks like we're here for a while."

"Oh great," the Princess moaned.

"Oh, you won't be here, your Highness."

"What do you mean?"

"They're sending a prison ship to pick up the pirates, and it'll be accompanied by three frigates. They've modified one of the frigates with a royal cabin to take you home, ma'am. They're scheduled to arrive this evening."

"Well, that's good news and bad news," Ariadne said.

"How is it bad news?" Josh asked.

"Why darling, isn't it obvious? It's bad because I have to leave you behind with no female companionship."

"I guess you're not leaving Vallana, then," Josh said.

Ariadne gave him a look that would drop the tropical temperature a good 20 degrees. "Not on your life. I'll explain it all to her on the way back home, now that I have a translator."

Rodgers fidgeted a bit before saying, "Is there anything else, Commander?"

"Oh, no, Rodgers. You may go now," Josh said.

The Lieutenant made a hasty departure.

Ariadne moved back to Josh's side. "We don't have much time, darling. We need to make the most of it while we can." She threw her arms around his neck and was about to kiss him when a siren interrupted her. "What's that for? I thought the pirates were all under control," she said.

"They are. I don't know what this is about."

His ear bud announced the problem. "Commander, this is Blake. We need you up here at the ship right away. We have seven pirate ships inbound."

"I'll be right there," Josh said. *Phew, dodged another bullet, thanks to the pirates.* He turned to Ariadne. "The pirates are trying a comeback. You'd better get back inside the fortress. I have to get to the Ares."

"Do you think we're in any danger?" she asked.

"I don't think so. Between the Ares and the fortress's missiles I think we can handle them. See you later."

Josh ran to the fortress where a skimmer was waiting for him. He boarded, and they made it to the shuttle pad in the city in short order. Within 45 minutes he was standing on the bridge of the Ares with Blake filling him in.

"The pirates are spreading out to attack from all sides. I've alerted the fortress to stand by with their missiles, and our marines are manning the consoles. I estimate they'll be here in another 20 minutes."

Josh, you have no idea what you're doing, but maybe it'll be like one of my shooter games. Josh took a seat in the command chair and pressed a few buttons on the armrests. After several tries and a few hints from Blake he managed to change the large display screen to a tactical layout of the situation. Seven blips marked as bogies were converging on the Ares, but his icons showed all weapons ready to go and the fortress missiles in launch alert.

Let's see, that blip marked number one should be within our missile range now. "Launch missile at blip number one," Josh commanded. *Hey, not bad. Sounded like a commander to me.*

Blake leaned closer. "How many missiles, sir?"

"Er, ah, what do you recommend?" Josh asked.

"That one's a pretty hard target. It's marked as a six on the defensive score." Blake used a laser pointer to indicate a red number just below the target designation. "I'd recommend three missiles."

"Make that three missiles," Josh commanded.

"Missiles away," one of the officers at a wall display shouted.

Josh watched as the three tracks sped toward the target. He reminded himself there were six other threats out there and studied the next closest one. The defensive number for it was only three. He leaned close to Blake. "Can we take on number five with our cannon?""

"Yes, sir, but it'll have to be a bit closer to do that." Once more Blake used his laser pointer to indicate a red arc designating their gun range. "I'd say we should let the fort take care of number four then we can concentrate on turning to engage number seven and number two. Three and six seem to be hanging back to see where they can take advantage of any weakness on our part."

The missiles converged on the target, and that threat disappeared. A shout rang out from the crew on the control deck. "Looks like we got one of them," Josh said.

"The missile explosions blank out the signal for a few moments, sir. You should order the fortress to fire on target four now."

"Oh, yeah. Commander to fortress, fire two missiles at numbe4 four."

"A bit of overkill, but no problem, sir," Blake advised.

Josh noticed the defense number on target four was only two. *Well, better to be safe than sorry.*

Target five was now in cannon range. "Fire cannon at target five," Josh commanded.

"Shall we use main battery number one, sir?" a voice on the intercom asked.

Josh turned to Blake who nodded his approval.

"Yeah just number one," Josh said. The ship rocked in response to the big guns, but the target only showed minimal damage.

"Keep firing," Josh commanded.

Another cheer announced the arrival of the fortress's missiles at their target. When the display cleared, Josh saw number one was gone, and number four showed major damage. Number five was still advancing in spite of continued cannon fire.

"Number five's still coming on. Did we miss him?" Josh said.

"No, but he has strong shields. We just have to keep shooting," Blake said.

The Ares shook as one of the pirate's laser cannon struck the aft shields.

"What was that?" Josh asked.

As if in response to his question the officer at the defensive systems panel spoke. "We took a minor hit on the aft shields, sir. The aft shields are down 5%."

"Is that bad?" Josh asked.

"No, sir. We can protect the ship with 20% shields," Blake said.

"That shot came from target number two," the defense officer said.

Josh checked the display and saw that number two was inside cannon range. He turned to Blake. "We got any cannon pointing in that direction?"

"I'd recommend the aft battery, sir. It's not as powerful as the forward battery, but it should do the job. Number two only has a defensive strength of three."

Josh gave the command. "Fire all aft batteries at target number two."

"Yes, sir," the gunnery officer said.

Another shot shook the ship, followed closely by two more.

"Target four is firing at us, sir," defense said.

"Hit him with forward battery number two," Josh commanded.

"Yes, sir."

"Targets three and six still holding back, sir," defense said.

"That's good. We're about maxed out now. I wonder why they don't close in," Blake said.

A bright flash knocked out the display just as the ship pitched up violently and the lights dimmed. Blake was knocked to the floor, and lay there unconscious. *What do I do now? I need that guy.* "Get a medic for Commander Blake," Josh shouted.

"Missile hit on the port shields, sir. Port shields down 15%," defense said.

"Where did that come from?" Josh said.

"Target number five, sir. He's still coming on."

"Give him a missile," Josh said.

"Missile away," offense said.

"Hey fortress," Josh called.

"Yes, sir."

"Chuck a couple more missiles at target five and lay one on number two while you're at it," Josh said.

"We can only do two at a time, sir. We have to reload the launchers after two shots, and that takes several minutes."

"Okay, but make it as quick as you can."

"Number seven moving into cannon range, sir," defense said.

"Hit him with a missile," Josh said.

"Still reloading launchers, sir. Another five minutes."

Cannon shots were now hitting the Ares regularly, and the defensive officer continued to report shield deterioration. A cheer went up from the crew as a bright flash of light announced the demise of target number five. Shortly afterward, another flash signaled the end of number two.

"Targets three and six moving in, sir," defense reported.

"Turn around and give number seven the front batteries," Josh said.

The display showed the ship turning and two targets appearing labeled seven and three.

"Where's six?" Josh said.

"He's moved behind us, sir," defense said.

"Hit him with the aft batteries," Josh said.

"Yes, sir," gunnery said.

Cannon shots continued to pound the Ares, but defense

assured Josh the shields were holding.

"We're ready to fire, sir, but target five is gone. What's our new target?" the fortress reported.

"Hit target six with both of them. Our rear shields are getting a workout from him."

"Missiles away," the fortress confirmed.

The heavy forward batteries were taking their toll of target seven, but target three continued to pound away at the ship's shields.

"Missiles ready to fire, sir," the missile controller called.

"Fire two at target three," Josh said.

'Missiles away, sir."

Josh watched as the missiles from the fortress converged on target six. Number six made a violent turn to avoid them, but one missile scored a hit, and the target vanished. Target seven was no longer firing cannon, but the track of a missile appeared from that ship.

"Missile incoming," defense shouted.

Josh noted number three turning to avoid the missiles from the Ares. It wasn't firing any more. "Hard left to avoid that missile," Josh commanded.

The ship's maneuver knocked several crewmen to the floor, but the missile sped past without detonating. "Aft batteries commence firing on target seven," Josh called.

A cheer from the crew caused Josh to look up at the display in time to see number seven break into several pieces as it tried to join number three in fleeing from the battle. It was over, and Josh turned his attention to the medics working on Blake.

"How's he doing?" Josh asked.

"He's coming around now, Commander," a medic replied.

Blake shook his head and waved the medics away. "I'm fine, just knocked out for a bit."

"Better come to the sick bay and let us check you over, sir," one medic said.

"I'll be in later," Blake said. He rose from the deck and joined Josh. "What's our damage?"

"I don't know, but I'll call for a report." Josh punched the ship's intercom. "All stations report damage."

The damage reports showed only minor wounds among the crew and very little damage to the ship. The Ares docked at the orbiting port for repairs, and Josh returned to the planet's surface and Princess Ariadne. As he entered her apartment, she ran to embrace him and kissed him passionately.

"I was so worried about you. I watched in the command center, and the Ares was taking some pretty hard hits."

Josh pushed her away a bit. "I'm fine, and there were only a few wounded men and some minor structural damage. Is there any wine?"

Mom and Dad would kill me for this, but it sure tasted good the last time, and I think I was supposed to say something like that.

Ariadne turned to Gerda. "Bring us some of that good red wine, please." She led Josh to the divan and nestled down beside him. "You smell like you've been under a lot of stress."

Instinctively, Josh lifted his free arm and sniffed. "Sorry, it was a bit stressful. I'll go take a shower."

"Don't bother, it's not an unpleasant smell. Tell me all about the battle."

Josh covered the highlights of the engagement, but emphasized the small part he played in the outcome.

"You're just being modest," she said. "I'll bet if I asked

Commander Blake what you did I'd get a different story."

"Poor Blake, he was unconscious for a good part of the fight."

"Oh, was he wounded?"

"No, just knocked off his feet by a cannon blast. He's okay."

"Well now, we can take up where we left off before those nasty pirates interrupted us." She threw her arms around him and kissed him.

Not again, what excuse can I give her now? She says my blood's blue enough and all that, but somehow it doesn't seem right. I know. "Ariadne, I'm saving myself for my wife."

She sat back on the divan and stared at him. "That's supposed to be my line. Do you mean you don't want to make love to me until after we're married?"

"Ah, yeah, that's it. I got old fashioned values, or something."

"Josha, I can't believe what I'm hearing. Here we are in this island paradise, and you don't want to take advantage of it?"

"We can come back here on our honeymoon, if you like."

"Oooh, you're impossible. Go back to your ship."

His ear bud came alive. "Commander, we have the prison ship fleet on the radar. They should be here in two hours."

"Okay, I'll tell the Princess," Josh replied.

"Well, darling, we wouldn't have had time anyway. Your ship will be here in two hours."

"Two hours! I have to start getting ready right now. Gerda!"

The Princess went into her fast and furious mode ordering Gerda about and making sure Vallana was properly dressed. Josh just sat and watched—very amused by the female attention to trivial details, at least they seemed trivial to him. The two hours passed quickly, and Ariadne was now dressed in a very royal gown in the middle of three large trunks. Gerda had Vallana in hand dressed as a proper lady, but the native girl didn't seem to care that much for the attire. She ran to Josh, threw her arms around him and began babbling in her native tongue.

"Somebody give me a translator," Josh called. Gerda handed him hers, and Josh began to understand the girl's pleading.

"Don't let them send me away from you, my Sagata. I haven't even warmed your bed yet."

"You must go, my dear. I have to stay here and protect your people for a while, but I'll come to you as soon as I can," Josh said.

"I heard that," Ariadne said. "You remember she's just a maid, Commander."

"I must be your gunna. My uncle, the Chief, paid me a great honor in pledging me to you. I must make you happy."

"I understand, and you will make me happy in many ways when I return home, but now you must go with the Princess. I will be with you soon." *This is all I need, two women who want my body. I'm glad I'll get out of this game sometime.*

"I will do as you command, my Sagata."

Vallana left him and joined Gerda. Josh handed the translator back to the maid just as a crewmember walked in leading a contingent to pick up the Princess's baggage.

"The shuttle craft is ready, your Highness. We'll take the luggage now if you like," he said.

"Yes, go ahead," she said. "Gerda, you and Vallana go with

them. I want to say goodbye to the Commander."

The others left, and Ariadne moved to Josh and placed her arms around his neck. She looked at him with a mixture of sadness and authority. She shed no tears, but her eyes were soft and pleading though her voice was commanding.

"I expect to see you as soon as you're back home. I'll make sure there's no one to interrupt our times together then."

I guess I should kiss her goodbye. She can't expect any more than that right now. He embraced her and kissed her as tenderly as he knew how. "I'm sure the next time you see the Commander he'll be all you expect him to be."

Ariadne drew back from him a bit. "What a funny way to say it. What do you mean?"

"I mean, I'm not myself right now, but I will be by the time I get home." *He'll be himself if I ever get out of this game. I've been in it for days now. Everyone must be wondering where I am. I hope I'm not dead, and this is my new life, like the Hindus believe. I have to give her something as a token of his love for her, but I don't have anything.*

He looked down at the Mahiki, but decided it wasn't quite the appropriate thing for a princess. Then, he noticed a ring on the little finger of his left hand. It was very delicate for a man's ring, and he thought a woman might not think it too masculine. He removed the ring and handed it to her.

"Here, take this ring. It has special meaning for me, and I'll be sure to come back to it when my mission's finished." *What baloney. Oh well, I don't know why I felt I needed to do that, but I did.* He kissed her again, but more formally. "Goodbye, Princess."

She placed his ring on her middle finger then moved her

hand to his face and touched his cheek. "Thank you for rescuing me. I don't think I ever told you I'm grateful. I'll tell you a hundred ways when you come home. Goodby, my darling."

She pushed away and walked out the door quickly. Josh looked after her wondering if this was the end of the game. As he stood thinking the room began to swirl around him finally blurring into streaks of red and blue as he felt himself propelled toward a white light.

CHAPTER 11

Josh awoke back in Disney World just as his sled was moving into the de-boarding area. George stepped out of the sled from the seat in front of him, and Josh made his exit.

"What's wrong with you? Did the ride make you sick?" George asked.

"No, no, I guess I fell asleep," Josh answered.

"How could you fall asleep on that ride? It was awesome."

"I don't know, but I can't remember anything about the ride."

One of the cast members controlling the exiting passengers called out, "Sir, you dropped this." He moved to Josh and handed him a small stone figure on a rawhide leather thong.

Oh my god, it's my Mahiki. Was that real? "Thanks," was all he could manage as he placed the thong over his head and let the figure rest on his chest.

"Where'd you get that?" George asked. "You didn't have it when we got on the ride."

The little nuisance doesn't need to know about my adventure in the game. "Oh, I had it tucked inside my shirt when we got on. It must have slipped off during the ride."

George walked to Josh and pulled open the neck of his T-shirt. He dropped the Mahiki inside and stood back. "No you didn't. See how it makes your shirt bulge? I'd have noticed that."

Josh looked down and agreed his story was highly

improbable. "I guess I must have had it in my pocket and it came out during the ride."

"Jeez, I think I'd know if I had something like that in my pocket or around my neck."

"Hey, I was thinking about Carolyn Forrest when I bought it. It's for her. I was just confused."

"You're always confused when you're thinking about girls. I can't see her wearing a leather thong around her neck."

"I'm going to buy a nice chain for it, stupid."

They walked into the Florida heat and sunshine and let their eyes adjust to the sunlight.

"Where next?" Josh asked.

"Pirates of the Caribbean, Pirates of the Caribbean!" George squealed.

Josh took the park map from his back pocket and unfolded it. As he did so, a lovely girl approached him from a group of Hispanic teens.

"Excuse me, señor, where I find 'Small World', please?"

Oh my god, it's Vallana. It can't be her, but it is. "Vallana?"

The girl looked at him with a wary stare, and Josh noticed she was wearing the same mouse-ears pin he was.

"No, my name Valera." She lifted her hand and touched Josh's mouse-ears pin. "What ride you go on?"

"I just left Space Mountain, how about you?"

"I on Jungle Cruise. You go yet?"

"No, we haven't been there yet. We're headed for Pirates of the Caribbean."

"Okay, you tell me where 'Small World'?"

Josh consulted his map and found the attraction. He held the map for Valera to see and pointed to the location. "Right there. Up that way past the Tommorowland Speedway, around the Mad Hatter's Tea Party and on past Prince Charming's Carrousel."

"Oh, I see. Have fun on pirate thing." With that, she walked on, and Josh looked after her for a long time. *It was her, and she had the same pin on. She acted like she knew all about the crazy adventures. I wonder if this pin works on all rides or just one?*

"Come on, Josh. We haven't got time for you to chase girls," George urged.

"Okay, okay, it's that way." Josh pointed to their left.

They walked past the large statue of Walt Disney and Mickey Mouse and on toward the other attractions. When they reached the Aloha Isle, Josh called for a stop.

"I'm hot. Let's have something cold."

"Okay," George agreed.

They ordered the pineapple whip and stood in the shade to eat it. Once more Josh started as a group of girls approached. One of them was wearing a mouse-ears pin, and she looked just like Ariadne. The girls also stopped at Aloha Isle, and Josh approached the girl with the pin.

"Excuse me, but I noticed you and I've got the same pin." He pointed to his pin.

She looked up from her ice cream and smiled. "How about that? Where'd you get yours?" she asked.

"I was on Space Mountain, where were you?'

"Pirates of the Carribean. Funny, but you look familiar to me." She took a bite of her ice cream and studied his face.

"Did you, ah, have any funny experiences on that ride?" Josh asked.

"I didn't do much laughing, if that's what you mean." She

continued to study his face. "You have any on Space Mountain?"

"I didn't mean funny, ha ha, I meant peculiar or unusual."

"Well, if you'd like to go over there and sit down, we can talk about it." She used her spoon to indicate a nearby bench.

"I can't, I've got him." Josh nodded toward George who was too engrossed in his pineapple whip to listen in.

"I can take care of that." She moved to the other girls and whispered something to them.

"Sure, we can do that," one girl responded. The girls moved to George and surrounded him. One said, "Isn't he darling?"

"He is so cute," another said.

"I wish my little brother was this cute," the third said.

"We'd love for you to join us for the Swiss Family Tree House after our ice cream?"

"Why not?" George replied as he reveled in being the center of attention. Josh and the girl moved to the bench.

"My name's Josh, Josh Martin, what's yours?"

"I'm Ari, Ari Goldstein. You wanted to know about the Pirate ride?"

"Yean, what happened?"

"One of the Disney characters gave me this pin while I was in line. I got on the ride and suddenly I was someplace else and inside some woman's head. It was really spooky."

"Same here. Buzz Lightyear gave me my pin, and I found myself on a spaceship inside the commander's head."

"It's really silly. I must have fallen asleep on the ride and dreamed the whole thing."

"Were you captured by pirates in your dream?"

Ari moved back from him a bit. "How did you know that?"

"Tell me the rest of your story, and I'll tell you about mine."

"Boys don't want to hear about some silly girl's dream." She dug into her ice cream with more gusto.

Josh looked down at his cup. The pineapple whip was nearly liquid now, and he set it aside. "I want to hear it. I think you may be surprised when I tell you my story if yours is what I think it is."

"Okay, you asked for it. I was a princess sailing across the sea to visit a new land when pirates attacked our ship. My crew fought bravely, but the pirates were too much for them. They took me and my maid to their island hideout and held me for ransom, but I was rescued by a navy captain I'd always admired. He fought off a pirate counter attack but he had to stay there to protect the natives in case the pirates came back. I had to go back home on another ship, but he vowed he'd come to me when his voyage was over. Now tell me about your ride."

"Like I said, I was on a space ship, a battle cruiser, and we had to rescue a princess from some pirates. I managed to do it all right, but the Princess had to go home. The funny thing is the natives gave me a medal kind of thing for freeing them from the pirates, but the weird part is that I had the thing when I got off the ride. Here it is." Josh showed her his Mahiki.

Ari's face went pale and she set her ice cream aside. She opened her purse and removed a ring. "Just like me and this ring." She held it up for his inspection.

"That's it! That's the ring I gave the Princess in my dream."

"Oh god, Josh. We were in a dream together, but how?"

"That pin." Josh pointed to her mouse-ears pin. "It's some kind of magic that transports you into a dream world. Have you been on any other rides since the Pirates?"

"No, we were headed for the Jungle Cruise when the other girls decided they wanted ice cream."

"Do you suppose this pin works on all the rides?"

Ari fondled her pin and thought for a moment. "What if we went on the same ride?"

"I'd love to, but my little brother wants to go on Pirates of the Caribbean," Josh said.

"I know, let's meet back here again after our next rides and compare notes."

"Okay, it's a deal. They're not back from the tree house yet. We can talk 'til they get here. Where are you from?"

"I'm from Atlanta," Ari said.

"No kidding? So am I, what part?"

"Up North, I go to Pace Academy," Ari said.

"Wow, that's an expensive school. I go to North Atlanta."

"That's a good school too and not too far from mine. What year are you?"

"I'm a junior, and you?"

"I'm a junior too. Do you play any sports?"

"No, I'm not an athlete. I go more for computers and technical stuff," Josh said.

"That's okay, what do want to do after high school?"

"I'll probably go to Georgia Tech and get an engineering degree."

"What kind?" she asked.

"I don't know, maybe computer engineering."

"I hope you have good math grades. You gotta have good math grades to be an engineer, or so I've heard."

"Yeah, me too, but I get As and Bs in math, so I'm not too

worried. What do you want to do?"

"I was thinking about Georgia and a degree in business or accounting. My Dad's an accountant with Ernst and Young. He's a partner," she said.

"My Dad sells insurance. Pretty dull, huh?"

"My Father says there's honor in all work, and that people should do what they love and damn the money."

"That's easy to say when you got a lot of money. I worry a lot about making enough money to get by in today's world," Josh said.

"You won't have any problem with that, I can tell just by looking at you," she said.

"Would you like to get together sometime back home?" Josh asked.

"I'd like that very much."

At that moment, the girls returned from the Tree House with George.

"You wouldn't like the Tree House, Josh—no excitement," George said. "Let's get to Pirates of the Caribbean."

Ari leaned close to Josh. "Meet you here after our rides," she whispered.

"Sure thing," Josh said.

CHAPTER 12

Josh approached the Pirates of the Caribbean with a great deal of trepidation. He was curious to know if the mouse-eared pin would work again, but not too keen on another adventure in never-never land. They took their place in line and shuffled forward with the mob. As they approached the boarding area, one of the cast members approached.

"Do you want to use your pin on this ride, sir?" he asked.

So that's how it works. Once you get one, you can use it as much as you like. "Yeah, I think I'd like to."

"Very good, I assume you're ready for this one." He winked at Josh and stepped back down the line.

I hope Ari said 'yes' on her ride. Maybe we'll be together again.

They boarded their boat and set off. Again, Josh didn't notice the cast member pushing a button on his boat. Once more he fell through a tunnel of red and blue lights toward the same white glow, but this time he emerged on the deck of a square-rigged sailing ship. He was bent over on the deck rubbing the rough planks with a piece of hard soap. On either side of him other men were doing the same thing. A harsh voice from behind spurred him to greater effort.

"Lean on it, ye scurvy knaves. I want that deck t' shine like me peg leg."

He stole a sideways look at the archetype of a pirate. The man did have a peg leg, but he also sported a patch over his right eye. Josh was a bit disappointed by the absence of a hook and a green parrot, but otherwise, the image was correct. He rubbed harder and noticed that his hands were rough and calloused. The skin on his arms was a deep bronze color from long exposure to sunlight. *Wait a minute. Ari said she was a princess being held for ransom and she was rescued by her hero sea captain. If I'm a captain, why am I scrubbing this deck? Evidently, they keep changing the dream in these rides. Oh well, all I can do now is wait it out and see what happens.*

"Sail ho!" The shout came from above, and Josh looked up to see a man leaning out of a high platform, pointing off to the left.

"Where away?" the pirate called.

"Two points off the port bow," came the answer.

The pirate ran to the bow of the ship and pulled a telescope from his sash. He scanned the horizon for a moment before shouting, "All hands to the guns."

"That's us," the man next to Josh said as he rose from the deck and deposited his soap in a wooden bucket.

Josh followed the man's lead to a large cannon on the port side of the ship. "Heave away, Joshua," the man said.

I don't know anything about cannons. It looks like they're trying to move it into that hole, so I'll lend a hand at that. He grabbed hold of a rope behind another man and pulled when he pulled. Soon the gun was fully into its port, and the other men began to tie off the ropes to rings in the deck. He noticed a large number '3' painted over the port opening.

The men seemed to relax a moment, and Josh watched enthralled by the vista of another ship just over the horizon. The pirate ship was gaining on it rapidly.

"No time for daydreaming, Joshua, my lad. Get th' quiltin' up so's we don't get no splinters."

Where's 'th' quiltin'', I wonder? He stood for a moment looking around and scratching his head.

"In the quilt locker, over there, are ye daft?" the man said as he pointed to a chest where other pirates were pulling out large sheets of heavily quilted fabric.

Josh took his turn and found two large pieces painted with the number '3'. *These must be for my gun, I guess.* He lifted the first piece, and it was almost more than he could carry. He lugged it to his gun and started to hang it up by the large brass grommets.

"That's the right hand piece. By gum you'd think the lad never manned a gun before," the man roared and the other men laughed.

Josh moved to the other side and hung up the quilt. Another man tied it down as he ran to get the left hand piece. Soon it was in place, and he noticed he could now make out the people on the other ship's deck scurrying about to man their guns. A puff of white smoke from one their gun ports was quickly followed by the report of the gun. Josh was amazed that he could actually see the cannon ball hurtling toward his ship.

"Head down, lad. Do ye want ta lose it?" The man forced Josh's head below the rail just as the cannon ball splashed into the water a few yards away.

"Steady, men. Wait for my command to fire." The pirate captain now stood on the rear deck armed to the teeth and smiling broadly.

Another shot came from the victim ship, but this time it smashed into the side of the pirate ship. The impact shook the deck, but Josh held his balance.

"Aim for her rigging, men," the pirate captain called.

The man who pushed his head down moved to the rear of the cannon and began to turn a small wheel under the breech, raising the muzzle higher.

"Are we loaded with bar?" another man asked.

"Aye, the Cap'n always goes for th' riggin' first, so that's what I loads 'er with," the man replied.

Josh noticed the man now held a long wand with a smoldering wick glowing on one end. The wick ran back along the wand and dropped down near the grip almost touching the deck.

Looks like the things they light candles with at church.

Josh rose slightly to see the victim was now very close. He felt his ship turning slightly to line up the guns and heard the order.

"Fire as your guns bear!"

More shots pounded the ship as Josh watched the gun captain move to the rear of the cannon and sight along its barrel. "Stand clear, lads," he called as he touched the glowing wick to a hole in the breech. The gun belched fire and smoke as it recoiled back against the ropes. The deck shook as the other guns followed his in pounding the victim.

Josh peeked over the rail a bit to see the bar shot spinning through the air and ripping the victim's sails and rigging to shreds. One shot hit the rear mast and splintered a section, causing the upper part to fall onto the deck. He felt his ship turning again as the gun crew worked to reload.

"Get some powder, boy!" the gun captain called to Josh.

"Right away," Josh responded and noticed the rest of gun crew laughing at his response. He turned to see other crewmen scrambling down a hatch carrying buckets.

"Don't forget yer powder buckets," one of the gun crew called as he tossed them at Josh. The gun crew guffawed almost uncontrollably. Josh was surprised when the leather buckets landed at his feet. *Leather buckets? Come to think of it, if you're carrying gunpowder, you wouldn't want metal ones, would you?* He picked up the buckets and followed the other men below decks.

Young boys were busy scooping out powder from large barrels into the leather buckets. Josh secured his load and returned to the gun. He noticed the other ship's balls were falling into the sea short of their marks as his ship turned to bring the starboard batteries to bear. Once more the pirate ship closed on the victim.

Josh noticed his gun was now fully retracted and one man was using what looked like a huge Q-tip to swab out the barrel while another man ran a rod into the gun's touch hole. Another man was busy bringing more bar shot from a large hamper.

"Well, put 'em down, boy," the gun captain commanded.

Josh dropped the powder buckets to the deck, and the gun captain used a scoop on the end of a pole to pick up powder. He studied the black substance for a moment and used his knife to skim off a small portion back into the bucket. He moved to the front of the gun and inserted the scoop into the bore. With a deft motion he dumped the powder and pulled back the pole. Quickly, another man pushed a wad of something into the bore and rammed it home with another tool. He stepped back, and the man with the bar shot placed it in the gun. The rammer followed that action with another ram and stepped back.

"Heave her out, men," the gun captain said.

Josh grasped the same line he'd used before and the gun was soon back in firing position. The gun captain poured a small amount of powder into the touch hole and waited.

This time the starboard side took the pounding of the victim's fire, but Josh could see the ship was severely crippled by their attack. He also noticed some of the cannon balls were now hitting higher on the ship, and all the shots were not single balls. Smaller projectiles whizzed past his head, and he saw he was the only one of his crew standing up. He dove for the deck at once.

The pirate ship's next salvo broke the other two masts, and the victim began to go dead in the water, though it continued to fire. He felt the ship turning again and knew they would soon be firing another shot. He watched through the gun port as the crippled ship came into view. Once more the gun captain sighted along the barrel and fiddled a bit with the elevation wheel before calling to clear the gun. He touched off the shot and finished the destruction of the victim's rigging. The other guns fired canister across its decks as the pirate ship maneuvered into position to board.

"That's all for us now, lads. It's cutlasses and blunderbusses now," the gun captain called.

The gun crew moved aft to join other men drawing weapons, and Josh took his place in the line.

"I hear she's a rich merchant carrying a fat cargo," the man behind him said.

The man in front of him turned to answer. "That's a royal transport ship, all she'll have aboard is prisoners for ransom, but the haul'll be a lot better'n any cargo ship. Our Captain knows his stuff, he does."

"Maybe we can have the wenches?" another man said, and a chorus of jeers agreed with him.

A man handed Josh a large sword and a heavy gun with a large barrel. He was barely able to carry them away. *What do I do with these? I don't know anything about this kind of stuff. I guess I could shoot the gun and swing the cutlass around and look mean, but that's about it. I'd better check out how this gun works.* He inspected the blunderbuss and concluded that pulling back on the hammer holding the flint cocked it, then all he had to do was pull the trigger, but how could he do all that while holding the cutlass? It was then he noticed other men had also drawn leather belts they slung across their shoulders to hold the cutlass. He moved back to the issue point and found the belts in a hamper. With the cutlass stored securely, he could manage the blunderbuss with ease.

"To the starboard rail, men," the Captain called, and the pirates congregated there. Some men climbed the rigging to the high platforms with muskets and powder horns. Josh guessed they would provide sniper fire from there. As he waited, he began to sweat profusely even though a cool breeze blew across the deck. *Man, I've played these kind of games before too, but this seems so real. It's different when all you have to do is work the buttons on a controller. I'll just have to try to remember what my avatar does when I do it.*

The cannons were silent now, but the sound of musket fire and smaller cannon shots took the place of the deafening booms. Small balls sounded like big mosquitos as they zinged through the air, and some men fell to the deck bleeding heavily. It didn't seem to be bothering the pirates still standing, however, and the glint in their eyes told Josh they were anxious for the fight to come.

The ships ground against each other, and some of the pirates threw large hooks across the narrow space between the vessels as others swung to the victim's decks from the rigging. Planks appeared with large hooks on one end, and these were fed across the gap and jammed into place. The crew of the other ship did manage to dislodge a few, but an avalanche of pirates spread to the opponent's decks. Blunderbusses thundered on both sides and the clash of cutlasses provided a higher pitched harmony. The man behind Josh pushed him forward.

"Get goin' lad. The Cap'n 'll have you flogged if you turn coward," he said.

Josh crossed to the other ship, and saw the carnage up close for the first time. It almost made his stomach turn, but he moved forward behind the other pirates. *Better fire this thing.* He pointed his blunderbuss in the general direction of the fighting and pulled the trigger. The recoil nearly bowled him over, but he managed to sling it over his shoulder and draw his cutlass. He waved it about over his head and shouted encouragement to the others, glad no one was near him to pose a threat. The fight was almost over when a sailor appeared from the hatch on his left and ran toward him brandishing a nasty-looking axe of some kind.

Okay, you have to make sure he doesn't fake you out. Watch his eyes. The sailor feinted toward his middle, but Josh waited as he redirected his blow to the head. Josh sidestepped the swing and plunged his cutlass into the man's side. The axe dropped from his hand, and he turned as Josh pulled the sword away. He looked at Josh with mixture of rage and surprise for a moment before he collapsed on the deck writhing in pain. *I guess I'd better finish him off. He seems to be hurting pretty bad. Wait a minute, maybe he'll recover? Don't be silly, this is just a game, do it.*

Josh used the cutlass to cut the sailor's throat.

The fighting stopped almost too quickly. The pirates were rounding up the remnants of the opposing crew and sending their arms back to the pirate ship. Gangs of pirates disappeared into the hatches and companion ways to seek out any other possible opponents and to capture any passengers that could be held for ransom.

Josh sat down on a nearby hamper and looked at the dead sailor. The deck ran red with his blood, and he felt remorse for having to kill him. *Hey, buddy, it was me or you. I'm sorry I had to do you in, but that's what pirates do.* He snorted in disgust. *Why are you sorry? It's only a game. I know it seemed real, but it isn't.*

Loud protestations in a female voice interrupted his thoughts. He looked up to see several pirates herding a well-dressed young woman and an older, plainly-dressed lady onto the deck.

Ah, this must be Ari. Josh moved closer to the commotion and studied the younger female. *It doesn't look like Ari, but I probably don't look like me either. I have to get closer.*

Josh pushed his way through the crowd around the women and whispered to the younger one, "It's me, Josh. Is that you, Ari?"

She turned and swung her arm to slap him, but Josh ducked quickly, invoking ribald laughter from his fellow pirates.

I guess not. Too bad she's not part of this dream, but I'll see her after this is over.

"She's not for you lads to play with," the voice of the Captain broke in, and the pirates parted respectfully as he approached the lady. To the surprise of all, he bowed before her. "Princess Louise, I presume," he said.

"Well, at least your Captain knows the respect due a royal Princess," she said. She assumed a commanding air and looked down her nose at the pirate Captain. "I insist you take me to the nearest port so I may contact my father and resume my journey."

"The nearest port is Phillipsburg, and we would not be welcome there. No lady, we're bound for Tortuga where you'll be held for ransom—in the greatest luxury possible, I might add."

"My father will send the navy after you, and you'll find your sorry behind swinging from a gibbet," she said.

The crew laughed at her threat.

She drew herself up into a haughty posture and said, "What's so funny about that?"

"Pardon my men, Madame, but your father's navy has been chasing us for several years now, and they've had little success. If I were in your shoes, I wouldn't count on any aid from that quarter." He turned to his First Mate. "Install her highness in your cabin and move the other officers according to rank. As soon as the booty's aboard, un-grapple and sink her."

"What about her crew?" the Mate asked.

"Those who won't join us can put off in her lifeboats or go down with her as they wish." He turned to his scribe and collected a waterproof envelope. He handed it to the ship's Captain. "See this gets to her father. It contains my demands and instructions for delivery of the ransom gold."

"How can His Majesty contact you?" the Captain asked.

"He can't. I have no intention of negotiating with him or anyone he sends to seek me out. Just be sure you deliver my terms in a timely manner. Your little princess has only six months to live if the ransom isn't paid."

"You barbarian," the Captain said.

The pirate Captain laughed at the insult and called to the crew. "Step lively, my boys. We'll divide the spoils back home."

The crew cheered and began a sea song as they worked to move anything of value to the pirate ship. When all was aboard, they unhooked the grappling lines and pulled away. Josh could see the crew lowering boats and rowing away from their ship. Only three men joined the pirates. His gun captain called for the crew to ready the gun, and Josh raced to his position.

This time, the gun captain loaded ball shot and cranked the gun to a depressed position. At the Captain's command, the port guns fired at the waterline of the victim. In short order the target began listing to starboard before dropping beneath the waves, leaving only a patch of floating cargo and broken rigging.

Josh stood at the rail watching. *Those poor guys. I don't know how far it is to land, but I hope they can make it.*

CHAPTER 13

The pirate ship pulled into a secluded cove somewhere on the island or Tor tuga and dropped anchor. Josh left the ship not knowing quite what to do. *I'm certainly not the Royal Navy Captain destined to rescue the Princess, but what am I, and what am I supposed to do?*

He walked through the small village near what served as a fortress for the pirates. It was little more than a dirt embankment, sitting on top of a high hill overlooking the cove, but that's where the booty was to be divided later. He bought some meat on a stick from one vendor and some fruit juice from another. Natives on either side hawked their trinkets. He looked at several clever pieces of sea shell jewelry, but none caught his fancy.

One stall sold small, silver skull and crossed bones pendants hanging from a delicate silver chain. He had just enough in his purse to buy it. *I hope this is like my Mahiki, and I get to keep it back in the real world. I think Ari'd like it.*

A lovely Hispanic woman sitting in the doorway of a cantina caught his eye and smiled at him. Josh walked over to her and asked, "Are you Ari?"

"Señor, I will be anyone you like for two peso de ocho."

"I'm Josh, don't you recognize me?"

"That is a good name, but I see so many of you pirates, how am I to remember you when it's so long between your visits? Come in, Josh, and buy me some wine."

"No thanks, I guess you're not Ari." He continued toward the fort.

The woman called after him, "Come back to Maria if you don't find Ari."

The fort was already rocking to guitar music, tambourines and flutes as he entered the gate. Groups of men gathered around women dancing to Spanish songs. They shouted encouragement and bawdy suggestions which seemed to urge the ladies on to more exotic movements. He noticed several mud brick houses with thatched roofs inside the earthen walls and spotted his Captain dragging a reluctant black woman into one of them. She seemed familiar, and he moved closer to get a better look at her. He was too late, as the Captain slammed the door shut just as he was getting in range.

That looked like Ari, but I couln't be sure. Aw, it couldn't be her. That woman was black. He started to walk away when he heard the Captain cursing from inside the house and a sharp scream. He tried the door, but it was locked, and there were no windows on this side of the building. He walked to his right and turned the corner only to find another blank wall. The rear of the building featured a high barred window, and the cursing seemed to be coming from there.

"I bought you, and you'll do as I say or feel the lash. I have to get something to eat and divide the treasure with my men now, but I'll be back after that. I'd hate to spoil that lovely back of yours with a beating, but I'll do it if you refuse me again. Think about it while I'm gone."

Josh heard a door slam and a bolt being thrown into place followed by soft sobbing from inside. He noticed several barrels stacked nearby and rolled one over to the window. He stood on it and called to the woman inside, "Are you okay?"

"Josh? Is that you, Josh?"

Even in the dim light of the room, the lovely black woman was unmistakably Ari. "Ari?"

"How did you get from the Jungle Cruise to here?"

"I was captured as a slave in Africa and brought here. It was so horrible on that ship. The Captain pulled me out of the hold and made me his personal slave since he saw I spoke English. I was out of that Hell below decks, but the new one wasn't much better."

"You mean he, he..." Josh struggled to put the question politely, but Ari saved him the trouble.

"No, not that kind of thing. He taught me how to polish his boots, take care of his clothes and clean up after him. He said that as long as I was a virgin he could sell me for a good price in the 'new world'."

"How did he know you were a virgin?" Josh imagined several tests the Captain could run.

"Not 'was', I still am. He had one of the other slave women on the ship check me out."

That's nice to know, but a bit discouraging.

"What are you doing here?" Josh asked.

"A pirate Captain bought me, and you know what he plans to do with me after he divides the booty among his crew tonight. You gotta help me escape, Josh."

Okay, so this is my mission here. Better start figuring out how to do that.

"Got any ideas?" Josh asked.

"I found out there's a group of escaped slaves up in the hills. We could slip away and join them, then maybe we could get a boat and get to America."

"I don't know what year it is. Maybe America isn't there yet?" Josh said.

"I looked at the slaver Captain's log, and his date was 1643."

"Well, looks like America's not the place to go. Maybe we could get to another island in the Caribbean. I wish I'd have paid more attention in geography class. I have no idea where we are," Josh said.

"I don't care where we go as long you get me out of here. If I remember rightly from my history class, Hispaniola is just South of Tortuga. I think it's French these days."

"Well, we'll need a boat, and some supplies, but first, I have to get you out of here."

Josh tried the bars and one was a bit loose. "Hey, I think I can get one of these bars out. Could you climb up to the window?"

"I could pull the bed over there and get to it, I think."

"Good. You do that while I work on this." He remembered his knife and used it to dig away at the mud brick holding the bars in place. *Man, this stuff's harder than it looks, and that bar goes down a long way. Nothing to do but keep at it.*

He finally reached the end of the bar just as Ari's face appeared in the window. "How's it going?" she asked.

"I think I've got it." He yanked on the bar, and it gave way, spilling him to the ground in the process.

"Are you okay?" Ari called.

"I'm fine. Can you make it through?" He pushed the barrel back to the window and helped Ari make a head-first exit from her prison cell. When her full weight fell on his arms, both teens tumbled to the ground in a heap with Ari on top.

"Josh, I'm sorry, I couldn't help it. Are you okay?"

"I don't think any bones are broken, but I'm going to be pretty sore tomorrow. Let's get out of here." He started to go back toward the gate, but realized the folly of that course. "We can't go that way, someone might see you. We'll have to go over the wall."

A stockade of tree trunks made the inner wall almost vertical. A few ladders gave access to the platform at the top, however. "Up that ladder." Josh pointed to one of them.

They climbed the ladder to a narrow walkway between two gun positions. A pirate Josh guessed to be a sentry sat dozing against the gun on his left with a broad-brimmed sombrero pulled low over his face. A quick peek over the stone wall serving as a battlement showed the same slopping earthen bank he'd seen coming in. "This way," he said.

Climbing over the low stone wall was not difficult, and the pair hurried into the cover of some brush at the bottom of the hill.

"What now?" Ari asked.

"We have to get down to the shore and look for a boat. Follow me." He led her around the fort to the edge of the small town, and they soon found the only way to any kind of boat was through the village.

"We can't just walk right through there," Ari said.

Josh looked around and noticed a blanket hanging from a tree limb in back of one store. He took the blanket and wrapped it around Ari. "This'll be a little hot, but you can cover your face with it."

"What about you?" she said.

"I'm a pirate, who'll suspect me?" He snapped his fingers.

"I know." Josh rummaged through the trash pile until he found an empty whiskey bottle. He returned to Ari. "I'll pretend to be drunk, and you can pretend to be my whore. That should be a common sight around here."

"Oh god, Josh. How embarrassing."

"Look, you know you're not a whore, and I know you're not a whore. What else matters?"

"If you say so. Let's go."

Josh did his best imitation of a drunken pirate while Ari pretended to be pawing him like one of the many prostitutes in the village. People only laughed and wished Josh good luck as they passed. They were just reaching the waterfront when a commotion from the fort signaled the Captain had discovered his loss.

"Oh oh, they know you're gone," Josh said.

"Quick, get us a boat," Ari said.

A slavo of cannon fire cause them to look out at the harbor. Several warships were coasting into the cove with guns blazing. Explosions from the area of the fort soon confirmed the ships were firing at the pirate's stronghold. Boats filled with soldiers began to be lowered from the warships.

"We're saved, Josh," Ari shouted and danced with glee, throwing off the blanket and waving at the soldiers.

"You forget, I'm a pirate. They'll arrest me. Come to think of it, you're a slave, and they'll probably just take you to one of their plantations to be a slave there. What did you say about some rebels in the hills?"

"But, won't being captured by the soldiers end our adventure?" Ari asked.

"I don't know. I'd rather take my chances in the hills."

As the first soldier set foot ashore, Josh felt himself falling through the familiar tunnel of red and blue. He awoke as his boat was pulling up to the disembarking area.

CHAPTER 14

Josh awoke to his little brother's prodding. "Wake up. You've slept through this ride too. What's wrong with you?"

I can't tell the little twerp about this stuff. He'd want a pin too. "I guess I'm just sleepy today, besides, this stuff's boring."

As they stepped from the boat, a cast member approached Josh. "Did you enjoy the ride, sir?"

"Yeah, sure did. I wasn't sure this would work again." He pointed to his pin.

"It's effective for today only, but on as many rides as you wish. Thank you for being part of our beta test program. You'll be receiving a questionnaire by email in the next seven days. We hope you'll respond."

"I sure will. Is this going to be part of all rides in the future?"

"That's what we're considering, but it's still under evaluation. Thanks again for helping us out." He shook Josh's hand and walked away.

"What was that all about?" George asked.

"Oh, they just wanted to know about me buying that mouse pin, that's all."

"That's not what I got out of that conversation. What's going on?"

"Nothing for little shavers like you to worry about. Come on, I'll buy you an ice cream."

"I don't want any ice cream. I want to go on the Jungle Cruise."

"After we get an ice cream. I promised that girl I'd see her after this ride."

"Girls, bah."

Ari and her friends were waiting at Aloha Isle as Josh and his brother walked up.

"Hey, Georgie, want an ice cream?" one of the girls called.

"Nah, I don't like ice cream all that much," George said.

"Come on over here and tell us all about the Pirates of the Caribbean. I'll buy you a Coke," another said.

"Okay." George turned to Josh who was already holding hands with Ari. "I guess you two want to be alone again anyway."

George joined the other girls, and Josh led Ari to the bench.

"Thanks for rescuing me again," Ari said.

"No problem, that ride was a lot shorter than the last one," Josh said.

"It was really awesome to do it the second time and know what was going on."

"Yeah, you looked pretty good as a black girl, too."

"Thank you. You were pretty hot yourself, even with all those tattoos."

"I had tattoos?"

"All over your back. You had a ship and a lot of things about someone named Lizzie."

"I hope they're all gone now."

"Lemme see." Ari leaned close to him and pulled back his polo shirt collar. "Nope, all gone. You didn't bring anything back with you."

"Wait a minute," Josh said as he searched his pockets. "Yeah, here it is." He pulled out the silver chain with the skull and crossed bones pendant. "I bought it for you." He handed it to Ari.

"It's beautiful, Josh. I'll wear it always to remind me of our time together here." She slipped the chain over her head and let the pendant dangle over her throat.

"I need to get your email and cell phone number," Josh said.

Ari pulled out her cell phone. "I'll call you now, and you'll have it. What's your number?"

She called Josh, and he made sure his phone recorded her call. "Now email me." He gave her his email and confirmed that on his cell phone also.

"How much longer are you going to be here at Disney World?" he asked.

"We're leaving in the morning, but call me when you get back home."

"You can count on that."

George interrupted them. "Let's get over to the Jungle Cruise. Mom and Dad'll be expecting us for dinner pretty soon."

"I gotta go. See ya back home," Josh said.

"You can't go without this." Ari stood up and gave Josh a big kiss. "Remember what the Princess said."

"Sure, sure I'll remember. Bye for now." George pulled Josh away from Ari toward the next ride, but Josh turned and waved to Ari, who blew him a kiss.

"Girls, bah," George said.

CHAPTER 15

Josh and Ari exchanged text messages until they could make arrangements to meet back in Atlanta. As he drove to her home, he fingered his Mahiki, remembering the adventures that seemed so real during their time at Disney World. He'd forgotten all about Carolyn Forrest now that Ari was in the picture. *I wonder if Ari wears my pirate pendant. I think she likes me, but we haven't really hung out together at all. She sure is hot. I need to find out if she really likes me, or if it was only the Disney thing.*

* * * * * *

The next week Ari texted Josh an invitation to visit her home and meet her parents. Josh's father arranged for him to use one of the family cars, and Josh used the GPS to navigate to a plush neighborhood on Atlanta's North side.

Her house was quite impressive. It sat on a large lot and featured a circular drive of paving bricks. Old trees flanked the entrance to the two-story replica of an antebellum plantation house. He pulled up behind a bright red Mercedes sports car almost expecting a valet to appear from the neatly trimmed hedges.

Ari answered the door. "I saw you pull up. Come on in, Josh."

"Wow, your house is awesome," he said.

"Thanks, come on in and meet my Mom and Dad."

She led him into a spacious living room where two middle-aged people sat enjoying what appeared to be a glass of wine. They stood as Josh entered.

"Mom, Dad, this is Josh, the guy I met at Disney World."

Mr. Goldstein extended his hand, and Josh remembered his father's admonition to give a firm handshake but not too firm. "Pleasure to meet you, Josh," he said.

Mrs. Goldstein offered her hand also. Josh was torn between kissing it and grasping the delicate appendage, but he decided a handshake was best. He did think to soften his grip to match her daintiness. "Welcome to our home," she said.

"Josh and I have some work to do on my computer, if you'll excuse us," Ari said.

"You kids go ahead. You don't need to be around us old folks all night," Mrs. Goldstein said.

"Thanks, Mom. Come on, Josh." She led him upstairs to a large room obviously decorated to suit a girl's tastes. One corner of the room served as a study area, and a large flat screen monitor showed a fish tank screen saver.

"I have to show you this. I just got it from Disney World. You probably got the same thing." She sat down and moved her mouse to show a screen of emails. She called up the one from Disney World. "Read that," she said.

Josh complied and stepped back with a low whistle. "That's really eerie."

"I know, have you had any of those symptoms?"

"No, at least I haven't noticed it if I did. Have you?" he said.

"I think you'd know it if someone was trying to reach you through mental telepathy. I had the strangest feeling a while ago, though. It was like you were telling me to put on the pirate pendant."

"I was thinking about that on the way over. I see you're wearing it."

"I always wear it. I love it." She fingered the skull and crossed bones absentmindedly.

"Wow, I got that," Josh said.

"Got what?"

"Didn't you just say you'd like to kiss me?"

"What! I didn't say any such thing." She moved her hand away from the pendant. "We hardly know each other. Why would I say that?"

"I don't know, but I distinctly heard you say it."

Ari stared at him then slapped his face. "I do not have the 'hots' for you."

"Wait a minute," Josh said. "I didn't say it, but I was thinking that. We've got the telepathy thing that email was talking about."

"Oh my God. We'll know what each other is thinking, and they said it could last for a week." Ari's hand flew to her mouth, and she backed away from Josh toward the door.

"Look, we just have to be careful what we think about," Josh said. "I promise to behave."

Ari stood with her back against the door and one hand on the knob as she concentrated on Josh. "You really meant that, and you want to stay here with me because you like me and want to get to know me better. It's like we don't need to talk."

"You're doing a pretty good job of blocking me out. All I see in your thoughts are pink rabbits and unicorns."

"What are we going to do?"

"Well, being honest with each other isn't such a bad thing, you know."

"I know, but a girl has to have some secrets. It just isn't right for a boy to be inside a girl's head." Ari moved from the door and sat down on her bed.

Josh sat down at the computer desk. "Funny, I haven't been able to read your mind until I was here in the room with you. Maybe it doesn't work if the two people are far apart?"

"I sensed your thoughts about the pirate pendant before you got here. It must have some range."

"I was pretty close to being here when I thought that, so it can't go too far."

"This is very uncomfortable. I have to watch everything I think right now."

"I'm going to be honest with you, Ari. I think you're a fabulous girl, and I really want to be your boyfriend. I can't lie to you. I've got the same urges every boy has, but I promise to be a gentleman."

"You know, it's nice to be sure you mean that. I won't lie to you either. I think you're a nice-looking boy, and I know we'd have lots of fun together from what we experienced at Disney World and what I see in your thoughts now. I see you like science fiction books just like I do, and we both like butter pecan ice cream."

"Yeah, but I don't like sun-dried tomatoes or sushi." They fell into a fit of laughter, and Ari recovered first.

"Think about the movies you like," she said.

Josh concentrated for a moment before Ari laughed again. "You've got to be kidding. You like *Singing In the Rain*?"

"Sure, it's a classic."

"I didn't think boys went for that kind of thing."

"I didn't know you liked zombie movies."

"You've got to promise you won't tell anyone about that. I only watch them up here in my room when I can't sleep."

"I promise, but how can watching a zombie movie put you to sleep? I'd think they'd scare you wide awake."

"They're so lame and so predictable. I actually get bored watching them. What I really like are murder mysteries."

"I see that. It's your turn. Think of sports you like."

Ari sat in concentration for a moment.

"College football but not the pros, okay. Ah, hockey. That's a surprise."

"You like hockey too, but you're a Blackhawk fan," she said.

"And, you're a Penguin fan."

"This is really spooky, isn't it?" Ari said.

"I guess I figured you were Jewish," Josh said.

"I see that's not a problem for you. What would we do if we really got serious about each other with you being a Methodist, and all?"

"We'd just have to work it out some way. Would your parents object to you having a Christian boyfriend? Oh, don't answer. I see they wouldn't have a problem unless we wanted to get married."

"Yeah, but that's a long way off right now," she said.

"Yeah, we've both got college before we can think about that."

"You know, Josh, we've only been together a few minutes, and I feel I know all about you. You're really as nice as I thought you were."

"And, you're even more than I hoped for."

"I'll really be sad when this telepathy thing wears off," she said.

"Me, too," Josh said. He moved to the bed and sat down beside her. They looked at each other and both of them shrugged their shoulders before they kissed.

A new adventure for Josh Martin is beginning.

What's your next adventure?

Title: *The Adventures of Regen the Bremen*
- •: Author: M. L. Hollinger
- •: Publisher: TotalRecall Publications, Inc.
- •: Hardcover, ISBN: 978-1-59095-110-1
- •: Paper Back, ISBN: 978-1-59095-111-8
- •: eBook, ISBN: 978-1-59095-112-5
- •: Audiobook, ISBN: 978-1-59095-253-5

Regen is a Bremen. By nature he loves only his pet skeen, sensual women, money, and adventure in that order.

Regen is an earthy, pragmatic, drug smuggler who cares little for anything but money, beautiful women, and his own highly unusual pet. The animal is a skeen, and they are usually shot on sight for the pests they are. Most people marvel that Regen managed to tame such a nasty creature. On top of everything else, he named the skeen HITLER after a 20th Century Earth dictator with a personality as evil as any skeen's. Regen is a Bremen. Bremen are known for their tough exterior, sexual prowess, and their tendency to leap before they look. I hope you enjoy following this arrogant, self-confident, egotistical and narcissistic bastard through a series of adventures in disparate sectors of the galaxy.

Young Adult and Adult

Title: *Josh and the Cargan*
•: Author: M. L. Hollinger
•: Publisher: TotalRecall Publications, Inc.
•: Hardcover, ISBN: 978-1-59095-124-8
•: Paperback, ISBN: 978-1-59095-125-5
•: eBook, ISBN: 978-1-59095-126-2
•: Audiobook, ISBN: 978-1-59095-254-2

Science tells us the speed of light is absolute, but is it? If physical objects can't go faster than 186,000 miles per second, maybe something else can.

Josh Smith is your average teenage boy. His hormones are raging and he can't wait to have sex with a girl. He also wants to be a rock star, and has an amateur band of his own. One evening after band practice he learns his rich, eccentric great grandfather, Charles Evans Bastin, is dead.

When the will is read, Josh inherits one of Charley's ugly sculptures while his father inherits the rest of the fortune. Back home, Josh accidentally discovers his sculpture is a CARGAN, a device used for interplanetary travel as a ghostly presence called an ENTITY. He travels to the planet destination of his cargan and finds it's a very exotic place indeed.

Young Adult and Adult
Recommend Age 17 and above

Title: *Mauhad*
- •: Author: M. L. Hollinger
- •: Publisher: TotalRecall Publications, Inc.
- •: Hardcover, ISBN: 978-1-59095-104-8
- •: Paperback, ISBN: 978-1-59095-105-5
- •: eBook, ISBN: 978-1-59095-106-
- •: Audiobook, ISBN: 978-1-59095-272-6

A boy struggles to pass Mauhad, the manhood test of his people, and falls in love in the process.

Javik lives in a country surrounded by mountains and covered in old growth forest. His ambition is to become a warrior like his father, Tolda, but he must pass Mauhad before he can realize that ambition. When is father is killed saving the others in his raiding party, Javik despairs of ever reaching that goal without his father's training. Goldar, who led the raid when Tolda was killed, convinces the King to allow Javik to train with Tao Shan, the finest mentor in the kingdom. Javik finds himself among the sons of the wealthy and must adjust to the situation quickly. While in training he encounters a girl in the forest. She is Allana an escaped slave, but Javik falls in love with her. He convinces her to come out of hiding, and she teaches the sling to Tao Shan's students.

The First book in the Javik series.

Young Adult and Adult

Title: *Love and War*
- •: Author: M. L. Hollinger
- •: Publisher: TotalRecall Publications, Inc.
- •: Hardcover, ISBN: 978-1-59095-285-6
- •: Paperback, ISBN: 978-1-59095-286-3
- •: eBook, ISBN: 978-1-59095-287-0
- •: Audiobook, ISBN: 978-1-59095-288-7

Allana goes in pursuit of a crown, and Javik is trapped into an unwanted marriage before the fates conspire to free him from all obligations except finding the woman he loves.

Javik goes off the war. He gains glory and gold in the war but returns home to find Allana gone. He's dismayed when Dana tells him she doesn't want him to follow her. He's also promised Tao Shan another year of training. He begins the training, and Tao Shan gives him a bonus by letting him in on the secret of a magic powder (gunpowder) and the weapon called a hand cannon.

The second book in the Javik series.

Young Adult and Adult

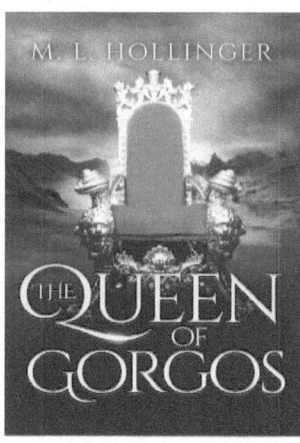

Title: *Queen of Gorgos*
- •: Author: M. L. Hollinger
- •: Publisher: TotalRecall Publications, Inc.
- •: Hardcover, ISBN: 978-1-59095-289-4
- •: Paperback, ISBN: 978-1-59095-290-0
- •: eBook, ISBN: 978-1-59095-291-7
- •: Audiobook, ISBN: 978-1-59095-292-4

Allana is held by the Turrek bandit King, Vargon.

Javik leaves to find her and learns of her predicament. With the help of her man Barinosh, Javik and his friends manage to free Allana and they set off to regain her throne. After many adventures Allana is crowned queen, marries Javik and they reign together.

Allana has begun her quest to regain the throne of Gorgos by establishing a high class brothel in another land with the help of a former madam who has been disfigured by a rejected lover. Allana gains a great deal of wealth and some allies, but she must cross the territory of a ferocious bandit king, Vargon, to reach Gorgos. She bribes Vargon with her body in order to secure his promise of safe passage, but he captures her in spite of his promise and forces her to marry him.

The third book in the Javik series.

Young Adult and Adult

www.ingramcontent.com/pod-product-compliance
Lightning Source LLC
Chambersburg PA
CBHW020529120726
47904CB00003B/1016